W. K. Clifford

Anyhow Stories

Moral and Otherwise

W. K. Clifford

Anyhow Stories
Moral and Otherwise

ISBN/EAN: 9783744750158

Printed in Europe, USA, Canada, Australia, Japan

Cover: Foto ©Andreas Hilbeck / pixelio.de

More available books at **www.hansebooks.com**

ANYHOW STORIES

MORAL AND OTHERWISE

BY

MRS. W. K. CLIFFORD

WITH ILLUSTRATIONS BY DOROTHY TENNANT

London

MACMILLAN AND CO.

1882

To my Dear Ones.

CONTENTS.

LIST OF ILLUSTRATIONS.

ANYHOW STORIES.

THE COBBLER'S CHILDREN.

LONG years ago, my children, all through a dreary afternoon a child sat in a garret working a sampler. Do you know what a sampler is? It is a bit of canvas on which are worked in cross-stitch some words, and now and then some little pictures. Long ago children were always taught to make them, so that when they became women they might know how to mark their table-cloths and pillow-cases and all the linen of the house, for in those days no tidy housewife had thought of writing her name in ink upon her belongings.

The child's brother was busy at the other end of the garret making a table. At Christmas time a great lady had sent him a box of tools; so with some bits of wood his uncle the carpenter had given him he set to work to make her a little table, just as a

5   B

mark of his gratitude, and to show her how useful
the tools would be and how well he meant to work
with them.   And all the time he was cutting and
fitting and measuring the little bits of wood, he was
thinking of a book his father had once read to him.
The book was written by a wise man, and the wise
man had said that he who made the first perfect
thing of its kind, no matter how small or simple the
thing might be, had worked not merely for himself
but for the whole world.   He left off for a moment
to wonder how this might be, and to think how grand
a thing it was to work for the world.   "It is a
beautiful place," his father said on the day they had
read the book together, " and a grand thing to think
we have all of us the making of its furniture."   Then
the boy looked up at the window and at the shoemaker's bench that stood by it, and at an unfinished
shoe, a little child's shoe, that was on the bench.
"Father takes so much trouble to work well," he said
to himself.   "He often says that when one does well,
one does some good to the whole world, for one helps
to make it better ; and that when one does badly or
does wrong, one does it to the whole world and helps
to make it worse than one found it.   But," he added,
"that cannot be so always.   How, for instance, can the

whole world know about a little shoe?" Suddenly he looked at his sister and noticed that the tears were stealing down her face, though she tried to hide them, and went bravely on with her sampler, working the figures that made her name and age thus—

SARAH SHORT,

AGED 7 YEARS.

He watched her and wondered. "If she works her sampler well, will it be good for the whole world?" And then he saw her tears again, and in a moment it seemed as if, of their own accord, his arms had twined round her neck.

"What is the matter?" he asked softly. "You dear little sister, why are you grieving?"

"Daddy is so ill," she sobbed. "He will never be well again."

"I will love you for him when he is gone," he said. "I will take care of you just as he did; I will take care of you all my life." Then, though her tears flowed faster, she was comforted.

"Oh, but I wish I could do something for him, because I love him," she cried.

The boy was silent for a few minutes, and stood thinking of all that their father had been to them. Then he said—

"We can't do anything for him now, but we will do things all our lives for him."

Then while the children stood still close together a woman entered. "You may come and see your father," she said. "You must tread softly; he is very ill." She looked round the room and saw the chips of wood upon the floor.

"I put the room tidy; you needn't have made such a mess," she grumbled; "I am tired enough." But the boy only heard her as if in a dream, and as if in a dream thought, "I will gather up all the bits by and by, and put the room neat and straight;" and then with soft steps and grave faces the brother and sister went to their father. He was lying on a little bed in the back garret. The children looked round at the whitewashed walls, then up at the little shelf of books above their father's head, then down at their father's face.

"My lass, is that you?" the cobbler said. "And what have you been doing?"

"I have been making this," she answered, and held up the sampler.

"And I have been making the little table," the boy said, answering his father's look; "it is a deal of trouble to get the bits to fit in and lie flat."

"Never mind the trouble, dear lad," the cobbler said gently, looking up at his boy's face ; it always told him what was in the boy's heart just as the hands of a clock told him the time that ticked and ticked away behind it. " Never mind the trouble, lad," he repeated ; "it's because you are sorry a bit to-day that you feel it. You must not think of trouble if you can only do a thing as well as it can be done— that is all the great men do."

" It's no use wasting his time over that table ; it is sure to be covered by a cloth," the woman said. " It would do just as well if he were quicker about it," and she left the room. She was a lodger in the same house with the cobbler, and was often puzzled at his ways.

When she had gone, the cobbler turned to his son again. " Don't heed her, lad," he said. " Do your best ; do it, lad, don't dream of doing it—good work lives for ever. It may go out of sight for a time ; you mayn't see it or hear of it once it leaves your hand ; you may get no honour by it, but that's no matter ; good work lives on ; it doesn't matter what it is, it lives on." And then, tired out, the cobbler closed his eyes and slept—so sweet a sleep, my children, that he never knew waking more. . . . .

The children were weary of sitting alone in the

twilight. They had nothing to say to each other ; they could not see to work, and the sister's eyes ached with crying, and the boy's heart ached with a still sorer pain.

"Let us go to the garden," he said ; and hand in hand they went down the stairs, treading softly and slowly lest they should wake the cobbler from his sleep. They sat on the stone steps that led to the garden—an untidy dirty garden, in which nothing grew save a little creeper planted in a painted wooden box. They looked at the creeper ; they could dimly see the tendrils struggling to grow up and up just a little way towards the garret window. They wondered if it would grow as high as the shoemaker's bench in the front room, and they thought of the little shoe their daddy had begun to make for the child whose name they did not know. The stars came out one by one ; the little sister's eyes filled with tears when she saw them, for it seemed to her that they had changed since she had seen them last, or else that she knew them better. They looked so soft and kind, as if they saw her and were sorry, perhaps as if they loved her just a little bit; and oh, they looked so wise, as if in that great far-off from which they shone all things were known and understood.

"Dear brother," she whispered, "I wonder if they see the little shoe, and Daddy's face and Daddy's books just above his head?"

"I can't tell," the boy answered softly, "but I think they know about them."

"Perhaps they knew Daddy loved us," she whispered again.

"Perhaps they did," he answered with a sigh, and then he said suddenly, "We have so many things to do; we must make a great many things and send them into the world, because he loved us."

"Wouldn't it have mattered about them if he had not loved us?" she asked.

"Oh yes, it would have mattered, he answered; "but I don't think we could have done them, love makes one so strong; it helps one to do and to bear so many things."

"Yes," she said softly, as they turned to leave the garden, "we must make the world a great many things and tell it Daddy sent them." She saw the wind stir the creeper in the painted box, and she said to herself, "Perhaps the little leaves can hear," and as she stood on the top of the steps looking up at the sky once more before she followed her brother into the house, she thought, "Perhaps the dear stars know."

THE NEW MOTHER.

I.

THE children were always called Blue-Eyes and the Turkey, and they came by the names in this manner. The elder one was like her dear father who was far away at sea, and when the mother looked up she would often say, " Child, you have taken the pattern of your father's eyes;" for the father had the bluest of blue eyes, and so gradually his little girl came to be called after them. The younger one had once, while she was still almost a baby, cried bitterly because a turkey that lived near to the cottage, and sometimes wandered into the forest, suddenly vanished in the middle of the winter; and to console her she had been called by its name.

Now the mother and Blue-Eyes and the Turkey and the baby all lived in a lonely cottage on the edge of the forest. The forest was so near that the garden at the back seemed a part of it, and the tall fir-trees were so close that their big black arms

stretched over the little thatched roof, and when the
moon shone upon them their tangled shadows were
all over the white-washed walls.

It was a long way to the village, nearly a mile
and a half, and the mother had to work hard and
had not time to go often herself to see if there was a
letter at the post-office from the dear father, and so
very often in the afternoon she used to send the two
children.   They were very proud of being able to
go alone, and often ran half the way to the post-
office.   When they came back tired with the long
walk, there would be the mother waiting and watching for them, and the tea would be ready, and the
baby crowing with delight ; and if by any chance
there was a letter from the sea, then they were
happy indeed.   The cottage room was so cosy : the
walls were as white as snow inside as well as out,
and against them hung the cake-tin and the baking-
dish, and the lid of a large saucepan that had been
worn out long before the children could remember,
and the fish-slice, all polished and shining as bright
as silver.   On one side of the fireplace, above the
bellows hung the almanac, and on the other the clock
that always struck the wrong hour and was always
running down too soon, but it was a good clock, with

a little picture on its face and sometimes ticked away for nearly a week without stopping. The baby's high chair stood in one corner, and in another there was a cupboard hung up high against the wall, in which the mother kept all manner of little surprises. The children often wondered how the things that came out of that cupboard had got into it, for they seldom saw them put there.

"Dear children," the mother said one afternoon late in the autumn, "it is very chilly for you to go to the village, but you must walk quickly, and who knows but what you may bring back a letter saying that dear father is already on his way to England." Then Blue-Eyes and the Turkey made haste and were soon ready to go. "Don't be long," the mother said, as she always did before they started. "Go the nearest way and don't look at any strangers you meet, and be sure you do not talk with them."

"No, mother," they answered; and then she kissed them and called them dear good children, and they joyfully started on their way.

The village was gayer than usual, for there had been a fair the day before, and the people who had made merry still hung about the street as if reluctant to own that their holiday was over.

THEN SHE KISSED THEM.—P. 10.

" I wish we had come yesterday," Blue-Eyes said
to the Turkey; "then we might have seen something."

" Look there," said the Turkey, and she pointed
to a stall covered with gingerbread; but the children
had no money. At the end of the street, close to the
Blue Lion where the coaches stopped, an old man sat
on the ground with his back resting against the wall
of a house, and by him, with smart collars round
their necks, were two dogs. Evidently they were
dancing dogs, the children thought, and longed to see
them perform, but they seemed as tired as their
master, and sat quite still beside him, looking as if
they had not even a single wag left in their tails.

" Oh, I *do* wish we had been here yesterday,"
Blue-Eyes said again as they went on to the grocer's,
which was also the post-office. The post-mistress
was very busy weighing out half-pounds of coffee,
and when she had time to attend to the children she
only just said "No letter for you to-day," and went
on with what she was doing. Then Blue-Eyes and
the Turkey turned away to go home. They went
back slowly down the village street, past the man
with the dogs again. One dog had roused himself
and sat up rather crookedly with his head a good
deal on one side, looking very melancholy and rather

ridiculous; but on the children went towards the bridge and the fields that led to the forest.

They had left the village and walked some way, and then, just before they reached the bridge, they noticed, resting against a pile of stones by the wayside, a strange dark figure. At first they thought it was some one asleep, then they thought it was a poor woman ill and hungry, and then they saw that it was a strange wild-looking girl, who seemed very unhappy, and they felt sure that something was the matter. So they went and looked at her, and thought they would ask her if they could do anything to help her, for they were kind children and sorry indeed for any one in distress.

The girl seemed to be tall, and was about fifteen years old. She was dressed in very ragged clothes. Round her shoulders there was an old brown shawl, which was torn at the corner that hung down the middle of her back. She wore no bonnet, and an old yellow handkerchief which she had tied round her head had fallen backwards and was all huddled up round her neck. Her hair was coal black and hung down uncombed and unfastened, just anyhow. It was not very long, but it was very shiny, and it seemed to match her bright black eyes and dark

freckled skin. On her feet were coarse gray stock-
ings and thick shabby boots, which she had evidently
forgotten to lace up. She had something hidden
away under her shawl, but the children did not
know what it was. At first they thought it was a
baby, but when, on seeing them coming towards her,
she carefully put it under her and sat upon it, they
thought they must be mistaken. She sat watching
the children approach, and did not move or stir till
they were within a yard of her; then she wiped her
eyes just as if she had been crying bitterly, and
looked up.

The children stood still in front of her for a
moment, staring at her and wondering what they
ought to do.

"Are you crying?" they asked shyly.

To their surprise she said in a most cheerful voice,
"Oh dear, no! quite the contrary. Are you?"

They thought it rather rude of her to reply in this
way, for any one could see that they were not crying.
They felt half in mind to walk away; but the girl
looked at them so hard with her big black eyes, they
did not like to do so till they had said something else.

"Perhaps you have lost yourself?" they said
gently.

But the girl answered promptly, "Certainly not. Why, you have just found me. Besides," she added, "I live in the village."

The children were surprised at this, for they had never seen her before, and yet they thought they knew all the village folk by sight.

"We often go to the village," they said, thinking it might interest her.

"Indeed," she answered. That was all; and again they wondered what to do.

Then the Turkey, who had an inquiring mind, put a good straightforward question. "What are you sitting on?" she asked.

"On a peardrum," the girl answered, still speaking in a most cheerful voice, at which the children wondered, for she looked very cold and uncomfortable.

"What is a peardrum?" they asked.

"I am surprised at your not knowing," the girl answered. "Most people in good society have one." And then she pulled it out and showed it to them. It was a curious instrument, a good deal like a guitar in shape; it had three strings, but only two pegs by which to tune them. The third string was never tuned at all, and thus added to the singular effect produced by the village girl's music. And yet, oddly,

"IT REALLY IS A MOST BEAUTIFUL THING IS A PEARDRUM."—P. 15.

the peardrum was not played by touching its strings,
but by turning a little handle cunningly hidden on
one side.

But the strange thing about the peardrum was
not the music it made, or the strings, or the handle,
but a little square box attached to one side. The box
had a little flat lid that appeared to open by a spring.
That was all the children could make out at first.
They were most anxious to see inside the box, or to
know what it contained, but they thought it might
look curious to say so.

"It really is·a most beautiful thing, is a peardrum," the girl said, looking at it, and speaking in a
voice that was almost affectionate.

"Where did you get it ?" the children asked.

"I bought it," the girl answered.

"Didn't it cost a great deal of money?" they asked.

"Yes," answered the girl slowly, nodding her
head, "it cost a great deal of money. I am very
rich," she added.

And this the children thought a really remarkable
statement, for they had not supposed that rich people
dressed in old clothes, or went about without bonnets.
She might at least have done her hair, they thought;
but they did not like to say so.

"You don't look rich," they said slowly, and in as polite a voice as possible.

"Perhaps not," the girl answered cheerfully.

At this the children gathered courage, and ventured to remark, "You look rather shabby"—they did not like to say ragged.

"Indeed?" said the girl in the voice of one who had heard a pleasant but surprising statement. "A little shabbiness is very respectable," she added in a satisfied voice. "I must really tell them this," she continued. And the children wondered what she meant. She opened the little box by the side of the peardrum, and said, just as if she were speaking to some one who could hear her, "They say I look rather shabby; it is quite lucky, isn't it?"

"Why, you are not speaking to any one!" they said, more surprised than ever.

"Oh dear, yes! I am speaking to them both."

"Both?" they said, wondering.

"Yes. I have here a little man dressed as a peasant, and wearing a wide slouch hat with a large feather, and a little woman to match, dressed in a red petticoat, and a white handkerchief pinned across her bosom. I put them on the lid of the box, and when I play they dance most beautifully. The little man takes off his hat and waves it in the air, and the little woman holds up her petticoat a little bit on one side with one hand, and with the other sends forward a kiss."

"Oh! let us see ; do let us see!" the children cried, both at once.

Then the village girl looked at them doubtfully.

"Let you see!" she said slowly. "Well, I am not sure that I can. Tell me, are you good?"

"Yes, yes," they answered eagerly, "we are very good!"

"Then it's quite impossible," she answered, and resolutely closed the lid of the box.

They stared at her in astonishment.

"But we are good," they cried, thinking she must have misunderstood them. "We are very good. Mother always says we are."

"So you remarked before," the girl said, speaking in a tone of decision.

Still the children did not understand.

"Then can't you let us see the little man and woman?" they asked.

"Oh dear, no!" the girl answered. "I only show them to naughty children."

"To naughty children!" they exclaimed.

"Yes, to naughty children," she answered; "and the worse the children the better do the man and woman dance."

She put the peardrum carefully under her ragged cloak, and prepared to go on her way.

"I really could not have believed that you were good," she said, reproachfully, as if they had accused themselves of some great crime. "Well, good day."

"Oh, but do show us the little man and woman," they cried.

"Certainly not. Good day," she said again.

"Oh, but we will be naughty," they said in despair.

"I am afraid you couldn't," she answered, shaking her head. "It requires a great deal of skill, especially to be naughty well. Good day," she said for the third time. "Perhaps I shall see you in the village to-morrow."

And swiftly she walked away, while the children felt their eyes fill with tears, and their hearts ache with disappointment.

"If we had only been naughty," they said, "we should have seen them dance; we should have seen the little woman holding her red petticoat in her hand, and the little man waving his hat. Oh, what shall we do to make her let us see them?"

"Suppose," said the Turkey, "we try to be naughty to-day; perhaps she would let us see them to-morrow."

"But, oh!" said Blue-Eyes, "I don't know how to be naughty; no one ever taught me."

The Turkey thought for a few minutes in silence. "I think I can be naughty if I try," she said. "I'll try to-night."

And then poor Blue-Eyes burst into tears.

"Oh, don't be naughty without me!" she cried. "It would be so unkind of you. You know I want to see the little man and woman just as much as you do. You are very, very unkind." And she sobbed bitterly.

And so, quarrelling and crying, they reached their home.

Now, when their mother saw them, she was greatly astonished, and, fearing they were hurt, ran to meet them.

"Oh, my children, oh, my dear, dear children," she said; "what is the matter?"

But they did not dare tell their mother about the village girl and the little man and woman, so they answered, "Nothing is the matter; nothing at all is the matter," and cried all the more.

"But why are you crying?" she asked in surprise.

"Surely we may cry if we like," they sobbed. "We are very fond of crying."

"Poor children!" the mother said to herself. "They are tired, and perhaps they are hungry; after tea they will be better." And she went back to the cottage, and made the fire blaze, until its reflection danced about on the tin lids upon the wall; and she put the kettle on to boil, and set the tea-things on the table, and opened the window to let in the sweet fresh air, and made all things look bright. Then she went to the little cupboard, hung up high against the wall, and took out some bread and put it on the table, and said in a loving voice, "Dear little children, come and have your tea; it is all quite ready for you. And see, there is the baby waking up from her sleep; we will put her in the high chair, and she will crow at us while we eat."

But the children made no answer to the dear mother; they only stood still by the window and said nothing.

"Come, children," the mother said again. "Come, Blue-Eyes, and come, my Turkey; here is nice sweet bread for tea."

Then Blue-Eyes and the Turkey looked round, and when they saw the tall loaf, baked crisp and brown, and the cups all in a row, and the jug of milk, all waiting for them, they went to the table and sat down and felt a little happier; and the mother did not put the baby in the high chair after all, but took it on her knee, and danced it up and down, and sang little snatches of songs to it, and laughed, and looked content, and thought of the father far away at sea, and wondered what he would say to them all when he came home again. Then suddenly she looked up and saw that the Turkey's eyes were full of tears.

" Turkey !" she exclaimed, "my dear little Turkey ! what is the matter? Come to mother, my sweet; come to own mother." And putting the baby down on the rug, she held out her arms, and the Turkey, getting up from her chair, ran swiftly into them.

" Oh, mother," she sobbed, " oh, dear mother ! I do so want to be naughty."

" My dear child ! " the mother exclaimed.

" Yes, mother," the child sobbed, more and more bitterly. " I do so want to be very, very naughty."

And then Blue-Eyes left her chair also, and, rubbing her face against the mother's shoulder, cried

sadly. "And so do I, mother.   Oh, I'd give anything
to be very, very naughty."

"But, my dear children," said the mother, in
astonishment, "why do you want to be naughty?"

"Because we do; oh, what shall we do?" they
cried together.

"I should be very angry if you were naughty.
But you could not be, for you love me," the mother
answered.

"Why couldn't we be naughty because we love
you?" they asked.

"Because it would make me very unhappy; and
if you love me you couldn't make me unhappy."

"Why couldn't we?" they asked.

Then the mother thought a while before she
answered; and when she did so they hardly understood, perhaps because she seemed to be speaking
rather to herself than to them.

"Because if one loves well," she said gently,
"one's love is stronger than all bad feelings in one,
and conquers them.   And this is the test whether
love be real or false, unkindness and wickedness
have no power over it."

"We don't know what you mean," they cried;
"and we do love you; but we want to be naughty."

" Then I should know you did not love me," the mother said.

" And what should you do ?" asked Blue-Eyes.

" I cannot tell. I should try to make you better."

" But if you couldn't? If we were very, very, very naughty, and wouldn't be good, what then ?"

" Then," said the mother sadly—and while she spoke her eyes filled with tears, and a sob almost choked her—" then," she said, " I should have to go away and leave you, and to send home a new mother, with glass eyes and wooden tail."

" You couldn't," they cried.

" Yes, I could," she answered in a low voice ; " but it would make me very unhappy, and I will never do it unless you are very, very naughty, and I am obliged."

" We won't be naughty," they cried ; " we will be good. We should hate a new mother; and she shall never come here." And they clung to their own mother, and kissed her fondly.

But when they went to bed they sobbed bitterly, for they remembered the little man and woman, and longed more than ever to see them; but how could they bear to let their own mother go away, and a new one take her place ?

II.

"GOOD-DAY," said the village girl, when she saw Blue-Eyes and the Turkey approach. She was again sitting by the heap of stones, and under her shawl the peardrum was hidden. She looked just as if she had not moved since the day before. " Good day," she said, in the same cheerful voice in which she had spoken yesterday ; " the weather is really charming."

"Are the little man and woman there?" the children asked, taking no notice of her remark.

"Yes; thank you for inquiring after them," the girl answered; " they are both here and quite well. The little man is learning how to rattle the money in his pocket, and the little woman has heard a secret— she tells it while she dances."

" Oh, do let us see," they entreated.

" Quite impossible, I assure you," the girl answered promptly. " You see, you are good."

" Oh !" said-Blue Eyes, sadly ; " but mother says if we are naughty she will go away and send home a new mother, with glass eyes and a wooden tail."

" Indeed," said the girl, still speaking in the same unconcerned voice, " that is what they all say."

" What do you mean?" asked the Turkey.

" They all threaten that kind of thing.   Of course really there are no mothers with glass eyes and wooden tails; they would be much too expensive to make."   And the common sense of this remark the children, especially the Turkey, saw at once, but they merely said, half crying—

" We think you might let us see the little man and woman dance."

" The kind of thing you would think," remarked the village girl.

" But will you if we are naughty?" they asked in despair.

" I fear you could not be naughty—that is, really —even if you tried," she said scornfully.

" Oh, but we will try; we will indeed," they cried ; " so do show them to us."

" Certainly not beforehand," answered the girl, getting up and preparing to walk away.

" But if we are very naughty to-night, will you let us see them to-morrow?"

" Questions asked to-day are always best answered to-morrow," the girl said, and turned round as if to walk on.   " Good day," she said blithely; " I must really go and play a little to myself; good

day," she repeated, and then suddenly she began to
sing—

> " Oh, sweet and fair's the lady-bird,
>   And so's the bumble-bee,
>   But I myself have long preferred
>   The gentle chimpanzee,
>   The gentle chimpanzee-e-e,
>   The gentle chim——"

" I beg your pardon," she said, stopping, and
looking over her shoulder; " it's very rude to sing
without leave before company. I won't do it again."

" Oh, do go on," the children said.

" I'm going," she said, and walked away.

" No, we meant go on singing," they explained,
" and do let us just hear you play," they entreated,
remembering that as yet they had not heard a single
sound from the peardrum.

" Quite impossible," she called out as she went
along. " You are good, as I remarked before. The
pleasure of goodness centres in itself; the pleasures
of naughtiness are many and varied. Good day,"
she shouted, for she was almost out of hearing.

For a few minutes the children stood still looking after her, then they broke down and cried.

" She might have let us see them," they sobbed.

The Turkey was the first to wipe away her tears.

" Let us go home and be very naughty," she said ;
" then perhaps she will let us see them to-morrow."

" But what shall we do ? " asked Blue-Eyes, looking up. Then together all the way home they
planned how to begin being naughty. And that afternoon the dear mother was sorely distressed, for,
instead of sitting at their tea as usual with smiling
happy faces, and then helping her to clear away and
doing all she told them, they broke their mugs and
threw their bread and butter on the floor, and when
the mother told them to do one thing they carefully
went and did another, and as for helping her to put
away, they left her to do it all by herself, and only
stamped their feet with rage when she told them to
go upstairs until they were good.

" We won't be good," they cried. " We hate
being good, and we always mean to be naughty.
We like being naughty very much."

" Do you remember what I told you I should do
if you were very very naughty ? " she asked sadly.

" Yes, we know, but it isn't true," they cried.
" There is no mother with a wooden tail and glass
eyes, and if there were we should just stick pins into
her and send her away ; but there is none."

Then the mother became really angry at last, and

sent them off to bed, but instead of crying and being sorry at her anger they laughed for joy, and when they were in bed they sat up and sang merry songs at the top of their voices.

The next morning quite early, without asking leave from the mother, the children got up and ran off as fast as they could over the fields towards the bridge to look for the village girl. She was sitting as usual by the heap of stones with the peardrum under her shawl.

" Now please show us the little man and woman," they cried, " and let us hear the peardrum. We were very naughty last night." But the girl kept the peardrum carefully hidden. " We were very naughty," the children cried again.

" Indeed," she said in precisely the same tone in which she had spoken yesterday.

" But we were," they repeated ; " we were indeed."

" So you say," she answered. " You were not half naughty enough."

" Why, we were sent to bed ! "

" Just so," said the girl, putting the other corner of the shawl over the peardrum. " If you had been really naughty you wouldn't have gone ; but you

can't help it, you see.   As I remarked before, it requires a great deal of skill to be naughty well."

"But we broke our mugs, we threw our bread and
butter on the floor, we did everything we could to
be tiresome."

"Mere trifles," answered the village girl scornfully. "Did you throw cold water on the fire, did
you break the clock, did you pull all the tins down
from the walls, and throw them on the floor?"

"No!" exclaimed the children, aghast, "we did
not do that."

"I thought not," the girl answered. "So many
people mistake a little noise and foolishness for real
naughtiness; but, as I remarked before, it wants skill
to do the thing properly. Well, good day," and before
they could say another word she had vanished.

"We'll be much worse," the children cried, in
despair. "We'll go and do all the things she says;"
and then they went home and did all these things.
They threw water on the fire; they pulled down the
baking-dish and the cake-tin, the fish-slice and the
lid of the saucepan they had never seen, and banged
them on the floor; they broke the clock and danced
on the butter; they turned everything upside down;
and then they sat still and wondered if they were

naughty enough. And when the mother saw all
that they had done she did not scold them as she
had the day before or send them to bed, but she just
broke down and cried, and then she looked at the
children and said sadly—

"Unless you are good to-morrow, my poor Blue-
Eyes and Turkey, I shall indeed have to go away
and come back no more, and the new mother I told
you of will come to you."

They did not believe her; yet their hearts ached
when they saw how unhappy she looked, and they
thought within themselves that when they once had
seen the little man and woman dance, they would
be good to the dear mother for ever afterwards;
but they could not be good now till they had heard
the sound of the peardrum, seen the little man
and woman dance, and heard the secret told—then
they would be satisfied.

The next morning, before the birds were stirring,
before the sun had climbed high enough to look in
at their bedroom window, or the flowers had wiped
their eyes ready for the day, the children got up and
crept out of the cottage and ran across the fields.
They did not think the village girl would be up so
very early, but their hearts had ached so much at the

sight of the mother's sad face that they had not been able to sleep, and they longed to know if they had been naughty enough, and if they might just once hear the peardrum and see the little man and woman, and then go home and be good for ever.

To their surprise they found the village girl sitting by the heap of stones, just as if it were her natural home. They ran fast when they saw her, and they noticed that the box containing the little man and woman was open, but she closed it quickly when she saw them, and they heard the clicking of the spring that kept it fast.

"We have been very naughty," they cried. "We have done all the things you told us; now will you show us the little man and woman?" The girl looked at them curiously, then drew the yellow silk handkerchief she sometimes wore round her head out of her pocket, and began to smooth out the creases in it with her hands.

"You really seem quite excited," she said in her usual voice. "You should be calm; calmness gathers in and hides things like a big cloak, or like my shawl does here, for instance;" and she looked down at the ragged covering that hid the peardrum.

"We have done all the things you told us," the

children cried again, "and we do so long to hear the secret;" but the girl only went on smoothing out her handkerchief.

"I am so very particular about my dress," she said. They could hardly listen to her in their excitement.

"But do tell if we may see the little man and woman," they entreated again. "We have been so very naughty, and mother says she will go away to-day and send home a new mother if we are not good."

"Indeed," said the girl, beginning to be interested and amused. "The things that people say are most singular and amusing. There is an endless variety in language." But the children did not understand, only entreated once more to see the little man and woman.

"Well, let me see," the girl said at last, just as if she were relenting. "When did your mother say she would go?"

"But if she goes what shall we do?" they cried in despair. "We don't want her to go; we love her very much. Oh! what shall we do if she goes?"

"People go and people come; first they go and then they come. Perhaps she will go before she comes; she couldn't come before she goes. You had better go back and be good," the girl added suddenly; "you are really not clever enough to be anything else; and the little woman's secret is very important; she never tells it for make - believe naughtiness."

"But we did do all the things you told us," the children cried, despairingly.

"You didn't throw the looking-glass out of window, or stand the baby on its head."

"No, we didn't do that," the children gasped.

"I thought not," the girl said triumphantly. "Well, good-day. I shall not be here to-morrow. Good-day."

"Oh, but don't go away," they cried. "We are so unhappy; do let us see them just once."

"Well, I shall go past your cottage at eleven o'clock this morning," the girl said. "Perhaps I shall play the peardrum as I go by."

"And will you show us the man and woman?" they asked.

"Quite impossible, unless you have really deserved it; make-believe naughtiness is only spoilt goodness. Now if you break the looking-glass and do the things that are desired——"

"Oh, we will," they cried. "We will be very naughty till we hear you coming."

"It's waste of time, I fear," the girl said politely; "but of course I should not like to interfere with you. You see the little man and woman, being used to the best society, are very particular. Good-day," she said, just as she always said, and then quickly turned away, but she looked back and called out, "Eleven o'clock, I shall be quite punctual; I am very particular about my engagements."

Then again the children went home, and were naughty, oh, so very very naughty that the dear mother's heart ached, and her eyes filled with tears, and at last she went upstairs and slowly put on her best gown and her new sun-bonnet, and she dressed the baby all in its Sunday clothes, and then she came down and stood before Blue-Eyes and the Turkey, and just as she did so the Turkey threw the looking-glass out of window, and it fell with a loud crash upon the ground.

"Good-bye, my children," the mother said sadly, kissing them. "Good-bye, my Blue-Eyes; good-bye, my Turkey; the new mother will be home presently. Oh, my poor children!" and then weeping bitterly the mother took the baby in her arms and turned to leave the house.

"But, mother," the children cried, "we are——" and then suddenly the broken clock struck half-past ten, and they knew that in half an hour the village girl would come by playing on the peardrum. "But, mother, we will be good at half-past eleven, come back at half-past eleven," they cried, "and we'll both be good, we will indeed ; we must be naughty till eleven o'clock." But the mother only picked up the little bundle in which she had tied up her cotton apron and a pair of old shoes, and went slowly out at the door. It seemed as if the children were spellbound, and they could not follow her. They opened the window wide, and called after her—

"Mother! mother! oh, dear mother, come back again! We will be good, we will be good now, we will be good for evermore if you will come back." But the mother only looked round and shook her head, and they could see the tears falling down her cheeks.

"Come back, dear mother!" cried Blue-Eyes ; but still the mother went on across the fields.

"Come back, come back!" cried the Turkey ; but still the mother went on. Just by the corner of the

field she stopped and turned, and waved her handkerchief, all wet with tears, to the children at the window; she made the baby kiss its hand; and in a
moment mother and baby had vanished from their
sight.

Then the children felt their hearts ache with
sorrow, and they cried bitterly just as the mother
had done, and yet they could not believe that she
had gone. Surely she would come back, they
thought; she would not leave them altogether; but,
oh, if she did—if she did—if she did. And then the
broken clock struck eleven, and suddenly there was
a sound—a quick, clanging, jangling sound, with a
strange discordant one at intervals; and they looked
at each other, while their hearts stood still, for they
knew it was the peardrum. They rushed to the
open window, and there they saw the village girl
coming towards them from the fields, dancing along
and playing as she did so. Behind her, walking
slowly, and yet ever keeping the same distance from
her, was the man with the dogs whom they had seen
asleep by the Blue Lion, on the day they first saw the
girl with the peardrum. He was playing on a flute
that had a strange shrill sound; they could hear it
plainly above the jangling of the peardrum. After

the man followed the two dogs, slowly waltzing
round and round on their hind legs.

" We have done all you told us," the children
called, when they had recovered from their astonishment. " Come and see ; and now show us the little
man and woman."

The girl did not cease her playing or her daucing,
but she called out in a voice that was half speaking
half singing, and seemed to keep time to the strange
music of the peardrum.

" You did it all badly. You threw the water on
the wrong side ·of the fire, the tin things were not
quite in the middle of the room, the clock was not
broken enough, you did not stand the baby on its
head."

Then the children, still standing spellbound by
the window, cried out, entreating and wringing their
hands, " Oh, but we have done everything you told
us, and mother has gone away. Show us the little
man and woman now, and let us hear the secret."

As they said this the girl was just in front of the
cottage, but she did not stop playing. The sound of ·
the strings seemed to go through their hearts. She
did not stop dancing ; she was already passing the
cottage by. She did not stop singing, and all she

said sounded like part of a terrible song. And still
the man followed her, always at the same distance,
playing shrilly on his flute; and still the two dogs
waltzed round and round after him—their tails motion-
less, their legs straight, their collars clear and white
and stiff. On they went, all of them together.

"Oh, stop!" the children cried, "and show us the
little man and woman now."

But the girl sang out loud and clear, while the
string that was out of tune twanged above her
voice.

"The little man and woman are far away. See,
their box is empty."

And then for the first time the children saw that
the lid of the box was raised and hanging back, and
that no little man and woman were in it.

"I am going to my own land," the girl sang, "to
the land where I was born." And she went on towards the long straight road that led to the city many
many miles away.

"But our mother is gone," the children cried;
"our dear mother, will she ever come back?"

"No," sang the girl; "she'll never come back,
she'll never come back. I saw her by the bridge:
she took a boat upon the river; she is sailing to the

sea ; she will meet your father once again, and they will go sailing on, sailing on to the countries far away."

And when they heard this, the children cried out, but could say no more, for their hearts seemed to be breaking.

Then the girl, her voice getting fainter and fainter in the distance, called out once more to them. But for the dread that sharpened their ears they would hardly have heard her, so far was she away, and so discordant was the music.

"Your new mother is coming. She is already on her way ; but she only walks slowly, for her tail is rather long, and her spectacles are left behind; but she is coming, she is coming — coming — coming."

The last word died away; it was the last one they ever heard the village girl utter. On she went, dancing on; and on followed the man, they could see that he was still playing, but they could no longer hear the sound of his flute ; and on went the dogs round and round and round. On they all went, farther and farther away, till they were separate things no more, till they were just a confused mass of faded colour, till they were a dark misty object that nothing could define, till they had vanished altogether,—altogether and for ever.

Then the children turned, and looked at each other and at the little cottage home, that only a week before had been so bright and happy, so cosy and so spotless. The fire was out, and the water was still among the cinders ; the baking-dish and cake-tin, the fish-slice and the saucepan lid, which the dear mother used to spend so much time in rubbing, were all pulled down from the nails on which they had hung so long, and were lying on the floor. And there was the clock all broken and spoilt, the little picture upon its face could be seen no more; and though it sometimes struck a stray hour, it was with the tone of a clock whose hours are numbered. And there was the baby's high chair, but no little baby to sit in it ; there was the cupboard on the wall, and never a sweet loaf on its shelf ; and there were the broken mugs, and the bits of bread tossed about, and the greasy boards which the mother had knelt down to scrub until they were white as snow. In the midst of all stood the children, looking at the wreck they had made, their hearts aching, their eyes blinded with tears, and their poor little hands clasped together in their misery.

" Oh, what shall we do?" cried Blue-Eyes. " I wish we had never seen the village girl and the nasty, nasty peardrum."

" Surely mother will come back," sobbed the Turkey. " I am sure we shall die if she doesn't come back."

" I don't know what we shall do if the new mother comes," cried Blue-Eyes. " I shall never, never like any other mother. I don't know what we shall do if that dreadful mother comes."

" We won't let her in," said the Turkey.

" But perhaps she'll walk in," sobbed Blue-Eyes.

Then Turkey stopped crying for a minute, to think what should be done.

" We will bolt the door," she said, " and shut the window; and we won't take any notice when she knocks."

So they bolted the door, and shut the window, and fastened it. And then, in spite of all they had said, they felt naughty again, and longed after the little man and woman they had never seen, far more than after the mother who had loved them all their lives. But then they did not really believe that their own mother would not come back, or that any new mother would take her place.

When it was dinner-time, they were very hungry, but they could only find some stale bread, and they had to be content with it.

"Oh, I wish we had heard the little woman's secret," cried the Turkey; "I wouldn't have cared then."

All through the afternoon they sat watching and listening for fear of the new mother; but they saw and heard nothing of her, and gradually they became less and less afraid lest she should come. Then they thought that perhaps when it was dark their own dear mother would come home; and perhaps if they asked her to forgive them she would. And then Blue-Eyes thought that if their mother did come she would be very cold, so they crept out at the back door and gathered in some wood, and at last, for the grate was wet, and it was a great deal of trouble to manage it, they made a fire. When they saw the bright fire burning, and the little flames leaping and playing among the wood and coal, they began to be happy again, and to feel certain that their own mother would return; and the sight of the pleasant fire reminded them of all the times she had waited for them to come from the post-office, and of how she had welcomed them, and comforted them, and given them nice warm tea and sweet bread, and talked to them. Oh, how sorry they were they had been naughty, and all for that nasty village girl! They did not care a bit about the little man and woman now, or want to hear the secret.

They fetched a pail of water and washed the floor; they found some rag, and rubbed the tins till they looked bright again, and, putting a footstool on a chair, they got up on it very carefully and hung up the things in their places; and then they picked up the broken mugs and made the room as neat as they could, till it looked more and more as if the dear mother's hands had been busy about it. They felt more and more certain she would return, she and the dear little baby together, and they thought they would set the tea-things for her, just as she had so often set them for her naughty children. They took down the tea-tray, and got out the cups, and put the kettle on the fire to boil, and made everything look as home-like as they could. There was no sweet loaf to put on the table, but perhaps the mother would bring something from the village, they thought. At last all was ready, and Blue-Eyes and the Turkey washed their faces and their hands, and then sat and waited, for of course they did not believe what the village girl had said about their mother sailing away.

Suddenly, while they were sitting by the fire, they heard a sound as of something heavy being dragged along the ground outside, and then there was a loud and terrible knocking at the door. The children felt their hearts stand still. They knew it could not be their own mother, for she would have turned the handle and tried to come in without any knocking at all.

"Oh, Turkey!" whispered Blue-Eyes, "if it should be the new mother, what shall we do?"

"We won't let her in," whispered the Turkey, for she was afraid to speak aloud, and again there came a long and loud and terrible knocking at the door.

"What shall we do? oh, what shall we do?" cried the children, in despair. "Oh, go away!" they called out. "Go away; we won't let you in; we will never be naughty any more; go away, go away!"

But again there came a loud and terrible knocking.

"She'll break the door if she knocks so hard," cried Blue-Eyes.

"Go and put your back to it," whispered the Turkey, "and I'll peep out of the window and try to see if it is really the new mother."

So in fear and trembling Blue-Eyes put her back against the door, and the Turkey went to the window, and, pressing her face against one side of the frame, peeped out. She could just see a black satin poke bonnet with a frill round the edge, and a long bony arm carrying a black leather bag. From beneath the bonnet there flashed a strange bright light, and Turkey's heart sank and her cheeks turned pale, for she knew it was the flashing of two glass eyes. She crept up to Blue-Eyes. " It is—it is—it is !" she whispered, her voice shaking with fear, " it is the new mother ! She has come, and brought her luggage in a black leather bag that is hanging on her arm !"

" Oh, what shall we do ? " wept Blue-Eyes; and again there was the terrible knocking.

" Come and put your back against the door too, Turkey," cried Blue-Eyes; " I am afraid it will break."

So together they stood with their two little backs against the door. There was a long pause. They thought perhaps the new mother had made up her mind that there was no one at home to let her in, and would go away, but presently the two children heard through the thin wooden door the new mother move a little, and then say to herself—" I must break open the door with my tail."

For one terrible moment all was still, but in it the children could almost hear her lift up her tail, and then, with a fearful blow, the little painted door was cracked and splintered.

With a shriek the children darted from the spot and fled through the cottage, and out at the back door into the forest beyond. All night long they stayed in the darkness and the cold, and all the next day and the next, and all through the cold, dreary days and the long dark nights that followed.

They are there still, my children. All through the long weeks and months have they been there, with only green rushes for their pillows and only the brown dead leaves to cover them, feeding on the wild strawberries in the summer, or on the nuts when they hang green; on the blackberries when they are no longer sour in the autumn, and in the winter on the little red berries that ripen in the snow. They wander about among the tall dark firs or beneath the great trees beyond. Sometimes they stay to rest beside the little pool near the copse where the ferns grow thickest, and they long and long, with a longing that is greater than words can say, to see their own dear mother again, just once again, to tell her that they'll be good for evermore—just once again.

And still the new mother stays in the little cottage, but the windows are closed and the doors are shut, and no one knows what the inside looks like. Now and then, when the darkness has fallen and the night is still, hand in hand Blue-Eyes and the Turkey creep up near to the home in which they once were so happy, and with beating hearts they watch and listen; sometimes a blinding flash comes through the window, and they know it is the light from the new mother's glass eyes, or they hear a strange muffled noise, and they know it is the sound of her wooden tail as she drags it along the floor.

ROUND THE RABBIT HOLES.

THE corn was growing up ever so high, and the poppies were red between. At the end of the corn-field there was a stile, and the boy sat on it watching the sun sink lower and lower into the west. "It is looking down on some wonderful city," he thought; "it sees the faces of the men and women glad to welcome it, and ready to work in the new light day, while for us there is only the night. It is a fine thing to be the sun; how grand it would be if one could journey on and on in front of it, with the day for ever before one and the night for ever behind!" He heard the children's voices in the distance calling to him, and he answered, "I am here, I am here; come and sit by me." And they came, saying—

"Tell us a story, tell us of the things you will some day do."

"Some day," he said with a sigh, "some day perhaps I shall journey to the strange city to which the sun goes at night. It must be a wonderful city, for, when the great gates in the west open for the sun to pass in, all the sky reddens at the sight of its beauty. Some day when I journey there I shall make all manner of things. I want to make them," he added, and sighed again, "for my father's sake, and for my little sister, who is far away in the town waiting for news of them."

"When do you mean to begin?" the children asked.

"I do not know yet. I have to work all day now for my uncle, and when it is over my hands are tired, and I have so much to think about; besides, I can make nothing yet so well as I mean to make it. I like to sit and dream of the days that will come; they will all come, but it's long to wait."

"How long have you been waiting?"

"Ever since Daddy died," he answered.

"Tell us about him," they said, though they had heard many times before. They were never tired of listening to the strange boy that had come to the carpenter's. "Tell us about him and about the little sister;" and the children gathered closer round him, and the tall girl with the pink apron, whose eyes seemed to know some strange language her lips had

E

not yet learnt to speak, drew up closer than the rest, so that she might lose no word of what he said.

"Nurse me," the little one said. Then the girl gathered the little one of three years old upon her lap, and sat on the lower step of the stile, and looked up at the boy's face while he spoke.

"Daddy used to make shoes and mend them," the boy said; "and he and the little sister and I lived in the garret at the top of a house in the town. In the evening, when Daddy had done his work, he used to sit and tell us stories: he told us about all manner of things, of all we must do, and of how the great men were those who did things as best they could be done. It makes one long to do things well so much; I will never do them badly, that is why I am waiting," he added softly.

"But one has to try one's 'prentice hand," the mother said. She had come to seek her children, but the boy had not noticed her. "One can but do one's best," she added sadly, "or maybe one gets no time for anything, and goes away as useless as one came." But the boy did not heed her, and went on—

"The little sister used to sit and work, for a woman in the house taught her how to sew, and she kept all the place neat, and tried to do the things

SHE SAT DOWN ON THE LOWER STEP OF THE STILE.—P. 50.

that would please Daddy, though she was only seven years old; and sometimes while Daddy worked at the bench she would sing songs to him."

"Ah, the little doers are better than the great dreamers," the mother said.

"And what did you do?" the girl with the pink apron asked.

"I always had so much to think about," he answered; "and then once my uncle came to see us, the same uncle with whom I am living now, and he saw the box of tools which the lady, for whose crippled child Daddy made shoes, had given me, and he sent me some bits of wood, and I set to work to make things. Daddy told me to be satisfied only when I had done my best, and to count all else as nothing, 'for when one did well,' he said, 'one did it for all the world.'"

"But one can get one's hand in by working for those about," persisted the mother.

"Go on," said the children, impatiently; "tell us about the little sister."

"She is with the lady who sent me the tools, learning how to do many things."

"And where is the little table you made?" they asked, though they all knew.

"It is in the great lady's drawing-room," he answered with a smile. "Some day I shall make a much better one, but I am waiting till I know more, and have thought of some grander way to work than I know now. . . . The night that Daddy died," he went on suddenly, "my sister and I went into the garden; we saw the stars come out, and we looked at a little creeper planted in a wooden box; it was growing up against the wall," and suddenly he stopped.

"Go on," they said.

"But that is all," he answered. "The little sister went to the great lady, and I came here, and am working for my uncle the carpenter, and am waiting—the rest is in my heart."

"Tell us what is in your heart," they said.

"I do not know yet," he answered. "One does not find out all at once."

"Now take us to see the rabbit holes," the children said, "and tell us all about the rabbits." So the boy rose to do as they wished, and the mother cried—

"Do not keep them out long; and see the little one does not fall," she added, speaking to the girl with the pink apron.

"I will carry the little one," the boy said, taking

her in his arms. The girl with the pink apron walked beside him, and the rest followed, talking among themselves as they went along. All down the cornfield they went, and over the gate with the padlock on it into the wood. Then soon they turned aside from the pathway and went in among the shadiest trees. The ground was thick with brake and briar and underwood, the nuts hung green on the branches above them, the blackberries were almost ripe on the bushes as they passed by.

"They are here," he said, and he stopped by a tree that grew at the farthest side of the wood, close to the hedge that parted off the hayfield. They could see the schoolhouse across the field, and the church, and they remembered the gate that stood close by the church and led to the village. The schoolmaster had stacked his hay, and the ricks were there right across the field, compact and well-shaped and comfortable-looking, ready for the winter; the children thought of the haymaking, but it was always nicer to be in the woods than in the fields. In the fields the green was only under their feet, but in the woods it was all about and above them, as if the sweet world wrapped them round and filled them with its beauty, till their hearts brimmed over with content.

The tree by which the boy had stopped was so tall and shady, it seemed as if the top that looked at the sky must be a long way off. "Here they are," he said. "I have never seen the rabbits, but I often think about them." The children went forward one by one and peeped into the holes, and the little one looked down at them, holding the boy tighter while she did so. Then they all stood in a group waiting for the boy to speak.

"Tell us what they do when they come out of their holes," they said.

"I don't know," the boy answered. "I have never seen them."

"What do you think they do?"

"I think that when the wood is still, and not a sound or voice or footstep can be heard, they peep out, and if they hear and see no one, they come out gaily and play about among the ferns and grass until they are tired, and they give little, short, quick runs, stopping to nibble a leaf or to listen to some strange sound, or else they stay still a while just to drink in, without knowing anything about them, the sweetness of the air, and the brightness of the sun, and the silence of the shade, and the little cool breeze that steals among the leaves and passes on."

"And what do they do at night?"

"Ah, at night they have fine fun. They scamper across the hayfield, running ever so swiftly, with their ears put back, and their little tails shaking, till they find their way into the schoolmaster's garden, and they eat the cool, crisp lettuce leaves, and play at hide-and-seek among the cabbages, and then they scamper to the hayfield again, and wander by the hedge back to the wood, and there they play about till the long gray dawn grows lighter and lighter."

"Surely you would like to see them?" the girl with the apron said.

"No," said the boy. I can think about them. I should not like them better if I saw them, and they might go and I should miss them. The things one thinks about stay unless one sends them away, and they never change unless one's self changes first."

"How did you learn to think?" the girl asked curiously.

"Daddy used to talk to me," he answered in surprise; "and it's just as if he talked to me still, or had written things down in a book. All the people we love teach us to see and hear."

"Do you love the people you don't see?" she asked, "for you love the things you don't see."

"Oh, yes," he said, "I love all people, they are so good," he added. "I have heard there are bad people, but I never knew any. All people have hearts, and if one makes for them one always finds them. But come," he said, "we must go home." And the children, not understanding what the boy and girl were talking about, turned silently round towards the gate that led to the cornfield. The little one's head drooped on the boy's shoulder, for she was tired. "You dear little one," he whispered; "my sister was small like you once, and I used to carry her in my arms down to the garden, and sit on the stone steps with her, waiting for the stars."

"The stars are in the sky already," the girl said.

"Yes," answered the boy, and he whispered to the little one—"The stars are coming out. They will all be out soon; they are shining down upon the little garden in the town, and the creeper is growing up to meet them; it will touch the garret window on its way."

THE THREE LITTLE RAGAMUFFINS.

THEY all stood at the corner of the street looking at the stall with the pine-apples, and at the man who was selling slices for a penny each.

"If I had a penny I would have a bit; I would have the biggest bit there!" said the first little ragamuffin. He was a greedy little ragamuffin, and liked big bits.

"It looks bad to take the biggest; I'd take the first that came," said the second little ragamuffin.

"I'd take the biggest!" said the third little ragamuffin; "for if I didn't, some one else would think me a fool for leaving it." And then they all went to the rail at the end of the court and turned and whirled and twisted over it and under it and all round about it, until their legs ached and their heads felt dizzy, and the palms of their hands tingled with excitement.

Suddenly the third little ragamuffin stopped, and sitting astride on the top of his rail, was silent for a few minutes; then he looked at his companions.

"There's Mary Lee been to the stall and bought a bit of pine-apple," he said; "shall we go and ask her how she likes it?" And in a moment they had all scampered up to her; but Mary Lee was afraid, and, dropping her pine-apple in the mud, began to cry, and ran home without it. And an old gentleman who was watching them caught the first little ragamuffin and boxed his ears; the second little ragamuffin picked up the piece of pine-apple, and, brushing the mud from it with his sleeve, ate it up, and thought how good it was; and the third little ragamuffin went back to the rail alone, and slowly and sadly whirled round it again. Meanwhile his friend was crying bitterly, for his ears had been boxed, and he had had no pine-apple.

"Please, sir," he said to the old gentleman, "we were not doing any harm; we were only going to ask her how she liked it."

"And the consequence was she dropped her pine-apple into the mud."

"Yes, sir, but she ought to have held it tighter; and I didn't get any, though I am very hungry."

"You look fat enough."

· "Yes, sir," sobbed the poor little ragamuffin, "mother likes us fat; but it takes a lot of keeping up."

MARY LEE BEGAN TO CRY.—P. 58.

" I daresay it does," the old gentleman said, and, pulling a sixpence out of his pocket, he gave it to the boy. " Here," he said, "take this; but let the lesson I have given you teach you experience. Do you know what experience is ? "

" No, sir," answered the ragamuffin.

" It is a thing that youth is eager for, and that age regrets, and that only a fool buys twice ; yours to-day bought you a box on the ear."

" And sixpence, please, sir." But the old gentleman turned away, and did not hear him. Then the ragamuffin bought six bits of pine-apple and carried them to his friends, and they all three sat in a row on the top of the rail and ate in silence, lest talk should spoil the flavour of a single mouthful. And when it was gone, the first little ragamuffin told his companions all that the old gentleman had said; while they, delighted at the feast they had, whirled round and round the rail for joy. But the first little ragamuffin sat up thoughtfully while he told his story, and pondered over it all.

" You see, Mary Lee, she lost her pine-apple and you ate it, and the old gentleman——"

' " He boxed your ears ! "

" And gave us sixpence ! "

"And then he said it was experience," said the thoughtful ragamuffin.

"Well, we say experience is excellent," answered the two little ragamuffins, whirling round faster and faster ; for they had eaten the pine-apple and found it good.   But still their friend sat thinking.

"Yes," he said at last, "experience is excellent; but it's best when another fellow buys it."

Meanwhile the old gentleman was walking home, for he had given away his last sixpence ; and Mary Lee was sitting in her mother's cottage, crying over her dropped pine-apple.

SHE SAT DOWN ON A BIG STONE.—P. 61.

FROM OUTSIDE THE WORLD.

SHE wandered about in the sunshine all the day long, over the fields and in the woods, picking the flowers and listening to the birds, and singing strange songs to the river. Suddenly she sat down on a big stone and looked up at the mountain that was just a little too tall for the world, and had to hide its head in the clouds.

"I should like to climb that mountain," she thought; "I want to know what there is on the other side." And the more she thought about it the more did she long to climb. At last she jumped up and washed her feet in a little stream of clear water, and set off as fast as she could for the top of the moun- tain. It was a long way up, but she sang all the time, and amused herself by wondering if any had ever been lost on the great hills around her,—the hills that stretched away and away as far as she could see,—and if so whether there had been wives and children watching for them at home, watching,

and waiting, and weeping, and listening for a footstep ·
that would never come over the heather again, for
the sound of a voice that never would speak to them .
more. "If I could only feel," she sighed, "if I could
only understand; oh, I would give the world to know
what it is like."

She went slowly down the other side of the
mountain. At its foot there was a little town; it
was just a very little town, with one street running
down the middle of it, and a town-hall in the
market-place, and a clock on the town-hall that
had lost its long hand, so it pointed to the hours with
its short one, and never troubled itself about the
minutes. There were not many people in the town,
but they all knew one another and talked about one
another, and nobody ever minded his own business, but
always some other body's. She stood at one end of
the street and looked at the schoolhouse and the toll-
bar in the distance, and she walked to the other end
and looked at the meadows, and at an old barn, and
at the farm-house, which was the last dwelling-place
she could see. "It is just the same here as every-
where else, I suppose," she said to herself. "The
people laugh and cry, and love and hate, and play
that queer game of theirs which consists in one person

gaining as much money as he can, and the rest getting as much of it away from him as they can, and the end of it is always the same; the man dies and is forgotten, and the next man goes on. I wonder what it all means." She sat down by the wayside and rested; she watched the people in the street, but no one noticed her. She saw two men pass by; she heard one say to the other—

"It is a fair price; that field is not worth more;" and she said to herself—

"It is the old story, they are talking of money."

A man and woman passed, the woman saying as she did so—

"I am not going to do it for less, I can tell her;" and again the girl said to herself—

"The old story, it is money for ever, money, money, for ever!" She got up and walked a little way, wondering if there were any children in the town, the children would be interesting, she thought. The old people were the world of yesterday; and the grown people were the world of to-day; but the children would be the world of to-morrow: of to-morrow that for ever was on its way, for ever held a promise. There was life in the very word, since only dead men ceased to think of it and to plan for it.

"There is some clue to life I have missed, there is something that I am longing for but cannot grasp. I am for ever feeling as if I ought to be paying myself in as a tribute to some great whole which I cannot see because of the darkness before me," she thought.

"Who are you, girl?" a voice asked suddenly. She looked up and saw a farmer behind her.

"I have come from a cottage over the mountain," the girl answered.

"What have you come for?"

"Just to see and to think," she answered.

"It is waste of time," he said gruffly, and turned away. "Will you have a cup of milk?" he asked suddenly, "for maybe you are tired; go to the house yonder, and say I sent you;" and he pointed to the farm-house. She was hungry and thirsty, and glad to do as she was told.

"Why do you offer me milk?" she asked; "I am a stranger."

"Strangers feel thirsty as well as friends," he answered.

The girl went to the farm-house, and when the good wife saw her she made her sit down, and fetched some fresh milk and home-made bread, and bade her rest well before she went on her way.

"I never gave any one a cup of milk or a welcome into my cottage in my whole life," the girl thought. "There is some meaning in the world I have not found yet, but it seems a little nearer as I sit and watch the farmer's wife." Then she rose, and, coldly thanking her, went on.

"I will go through the town now," she said to herself. A boy was sitting on the gate at the end of the field. He was gaily dressed : from his cap there hung a gold tassel, and on his finger he wore a ring. The girl stopped and looked at him.

"Where do you live?" she asked.

"I live at the great house up there," he answered, nodding in the direction of the hill. "You can see the flag waving from the tower."

"You must be rich," she said, "for your house is very grand. How did you get all your money?"

"My ancestors won it hundreds of years ago," he answered proudly. "They were great men."

"And are you great?" she asked.

"I am great, for I am rich," he answered.

"And so you have time to think," she said eagerly. "Tell me, do you know all things?"

"No," he said, "I never trouble about them; I am content to live and enjoy my riches."

F

"I cannot understand it," she sighed; "men are content to work for those they will never see, and to heap up money perchance for fools to spend. Money doesn't make you great," she said scornfully to the boy; "any booby can inherit."

She went down the street, she looked at the faces of the people; on all of them there seemed to be written some history of past days, some record of joy and sorrow, but most of sorrow. "I am very thankful," she thought, "that I shall never know the things they know. I remember once overhearing some poet or dreamer say that in every heart there was a death chamber; there is none in mine; I have no heart to hold one." The townspeople were looking out at their doors, laughing and making merry when any two met; she wondered what it was all about, till suddenly she saw a bridal party go by. "I see now," she said to herself; "these are two people going to marry, and they are rejoicing because they will be together henceforth. One will know when the other sorrows, and one will sit and watch at last by the other's dead face. Why do they rejoice? Oh! I shall never understand it all." She turned out of the street, and went towards the fields again. A boy was loitering on his way from school, and farther on there sat a man by an easel, on which stood an untouched canvas. The boy looked at the girl.

"What do you learn at school?" she asked.

"All kinds of things," he answered. "I am very happy while I am learning," he added. "And after the lessons come the games."

"What shall you do when you are a man?" she asked.

"I shall go on with the making of the world," he said, and began to sing.

"Why do you want to do that? We all die soon."

"It was made for us, it is ours now, we have to make it for those to come. Even to think of it makes one long to begin."

"But we shall not be here."

"Others will;" he laughed, and went on his way still singing.

"Perhaps the artist will tell me something," she thought, and went up to him.

"Have you painted many pictures?" she asked.

"No," he answered, "I have painted none that are worth remembering yet, but I shall some day."

"How do you know?" she asked curiously.

"Because I love the world so much," he answered;

"it is very beautiful," he sighed. " I should despair of my own self, but that love makes one so strong; it helps one to do all things."

" Why do you want to paint pictures?" she asked.

" Pictures are messages of light in dark places," he answered. " I want to tell the story of the world's beauty to the cities, so that some of those who live, and work, and have seldom time to rest, and never time to journey, may wander in its fairest places and know them in their hearts." The girl's face became eager as she listened, she felt some dim understanding, and yet why should he care for un- known people in unseen cities?

" And can you do it; can you make pictures that will do this, and where did you get the power?"

" I worked for it; I am working for it still, and some day I shall succeed, as all, who love their work well, must."

" Love—what has that to do with it?"

" One must love one's work," he answered. " 'For whatever a man loves he can create, and the work of his hands is that in which his soul delighteth.'"

" There is some use in love that makes the world prettier or better," she said; "I understand that, but there is none in love the end of which is parting and sorrow."

"The one is the outcome of the other," he said. "As death is the consequence of life, so is sorrow the outcome of joy, the price we pay for it somehow or at sometime."

"But if that is so," the girl said, "surely you should bear your sorrows in silence, and not cry out as if your happiness had been over-dear."

" Ah," said the painter, taking up his brush, " that is an easy thing to say, and a sorry one to hear;" and then he began to work, and the girl went towards the hill.

" I will go home," she said to herself; "I am no wiser than when I came." She passed a cottage at the foot of the hill; an old woman sat by the door knitting. Suddenly the girl stopped.

" May I come in and rest a bit, mother?" she asked.

"Yes, my child," the woman answered ; and she took the girl into the cottage and made her sit down by the fire, and gave her food and drink, and watched her while she rested. Suddenly the girl looked up.

"Mother," she said, "I have been wandering through the little town looking at the people, only

at the outside of their lives, and hearing just their
most careless words.   Tell me, what does it all
mean ?   Why do they go on eager for life which is
often a burden, and for money which none can hold
long ? ”

“ Where have you come from that you ask these
things ?”

“ I came over the hill this morning from a cottage
just outside the world, and so I have no share
in the world.   I am just a spectator.   But what
does it all mean—the hate and the love, the joy and
sorrow, the for ever seeking for happiness that
must for ever turn to woe in the end ?”

“ Surely we should be content to take our share
of work, and sorrow, and pain ; we that take the
world’s life, and light, and shelter, and sunshine,
shall we bear nothing in return ?” the woman said in
surprise.

“ And money ?   Does money bring you happiness that you seek for it, and bear so much for its
sake ?”

“ Seldom enough, dear, unless it finds other things
to keep it company.   There is nothing so overrated
in all the world as money,” the woman said.

“ Why do so many seek it ?”

" I cannot tell, dear lassie, for I never had it, or desired it ; but some is necessary, and all should be willing to work for their share of it, but more than this I cannot understand. Why it is so precious and so difficult to win, where so many are willing to work for it, is one of the strange things one has to think about. There are many better things than money ; it is a thousand pities so much good time is wasted in seeking it."

" And why do people desire to work; is it for honour ? "

" The best workers think only of their work," the woman answered, " and whether it will be good for the world and in itself, or of what it will do for others, not of what it will do for themselves."

" And love——"

" Ah," the woman said quickly, " out of good love and good work has the world grown up ; from them and through them we possess all good things. To love well and to work well are the two things to desire in life, for all other things are in their gift. To the lovers and the students we owe all things."

" But the world is not made up of these, dear mother; there are the soldiers, and the lawgivers, and many others."

"They have been lovers and students first."

The girl did not ask how this might be, for she thought of the words the painter had quoted, "For whatever a man loves he can create, and the work of his hands is that in which his soul delighteth;" and dimly she was beginning to understand.

"Why do people desire to do good work for the world which they hardly know and have scarcely seen?" she asked.

"The world is ourselves," the woman answered; "it is the thing we make it, and we can all help to choose what manner of thing it shall be for those who come after us. Even the least of us can help to root out sin, and to make unkindness strange, and some one life better because ours has been. Oh! my dear," she cried passionately, "if I could but hope that you and I may think this, and know it before the day comes when our hands shall be folded, and only our work shall say that we have lived——" But the girl looked on still wondering.

"How did you come to think and know all these things?" she asked.

"I have been alone so long," the woman answered, "just sitting by the fire thinking. But why are you going? stay a little longer if you will, lassie."

"It is a long way over the hills," the girl answered, "and I must go home to the cottage." As she spoke she looked back longingly at the little town, and at the smoke rising up from the houses in which the people rejoiced, and sorrowed, and worked, and lived out their simple lives. Then suddenly she looked up at the woman.

"Good-bye, dear mother," she said. "It is a strange thing, but I would give the world to put my arms round your neck and kiss you just once."

"And why not?" the woman asked, gently.

"I cannot," the girl answered; "something holds me back. I am just a spectator and have no part in the world, and cannot understand the things for which it cares so much."

"But why is that?"

"Oh, mother, I have no heart, and I live outside the world and have no share or part in it; its joys and sorrows alike pass me by and are never mine;" and she started on her way.

"No heart!" the woman said sadly. "Ah, poor lassie! then the world must indeed be a riddle of which you have for ever missed the answer."

THE PAPER SHIP.

I SAILED away in a paper ship,
   I sailed away and away,
And never did sailor sail so far,
   And never was sail so gay.
I sailed away to an unknown land,
   Beyond an unknown sea,
Where all the people were dolls, my dear,
   And all of them talked to me.

The town was built of card and paint,
   The gardens were made of tin ;
And dolls looked out at the windows, dear,
   And all of them asked me in.
And dolls sat round on the chairs inside;
   They all were dressed so fine ;
They stared at a clock that never had ticked,
   And was ever at half-past nine.

"What shall we do to be real?" they cried,
   " What shall we do to be real ?

We none of us feel, though we look so nice,
  And talk of the vague ideal."
And all of them seemed to know so much,
  But none of them laughed or sang ;
And none of the fires had ever a blaze,
  And none of the bells e'er rang.

And people walked and talked of life,
  And all of them looked so grave ;
Yet none of them ever had life, my dear,
  Or ever a soul to save.

I fled away to the woods and fields ;
  The trees were stuck with glue ;
And even the sky was false, my dear,
  And painted a lovely blue.
And dogs and sheep and cows were there,
  And all of them stared at me
With large glass eyes that never had blinked,
  And never a one could see.

I sailed away in a paper ship,
  Away on an unknown sea ;
And all the fishes were hollow, my dear,
  And all of them swam at me.

But on and on and on I sailed;
I met a great wet seal,
He looked at me with two dim eyes,
And turned upon his heel.

The strangest sail that never was sailed,
And sight that never was seen—
The sail I sailed in my paper ship,—
The land that never has been.

THE BABY'S LEGS.

BETSY's mother went out charing. All the day long she scrubbed and cleaned and rubbed at other people's goods and chattels, and at night, when she was tired out and could do no more, she went back to the two kitchens in which she and her children lived, and sat by the fire and rested. It was just the same, day in and day out all the year round ; but the good woman never grumbled, only thought what a blessed thing it was that long since she had spent some happy years with her good man gone .to rest, and that since then she had been able to work for the five little ones he had left her. Betsy was the eldest of them all, and eleven years old was Betsy, a thrifty little lass, able to scrub and clean, and mend and make, and to buy a dinner and cook it. " I never can think where she learnt it all," her mother sighed many a time when she sat down by the bright fire and clean hearth that awaited her in the evening, "except she's learnt it off her own heart.

She's never been spoilt yet, and it's wonderful how much good people are born with. The way they come by the bad is rubbing about the world."

"True enough, neighbour, depend upon it," the stonecutter's wife, who dropped in for a gossip one morning, answered; "it's a wicked world, and the sooner we get out of it the better."

"It's a very good world," the charwoman said, "if folks would only leave it alone. It's the people that spoil it, and mostly the grown-ups. The children are born good enough; it's the grown-up folk that prevent their keeping so."

"Maybe you are right," said the stonecutter's wife. "I always whipped my children well myself, and never stood any nonsense, and I'm very thankful to think it."

"You ought to be ashamed of yourself, Mrs. Jones, at your time of life to talk in such a way," the charwoman cried, and with that they fell to quarrelling and discussed the world no more.

Meanwhile Betsy had gone upstairs for the other lodger's baby. She minded it all the day long, as well as her own little brothers and sisters, for the other lodger was as poor as the charwoman, and also went out to work. Betsy took the poor little baby

in her arms, and went on her way to market all in
the morning early, so that she might be indoors before
her mother went out to work. Now Betsy had very
few clothes, and those were ragged, and she had little
time to mend them, for she had the children and the
baby to take care of, and the place to keep clean, and
errands to go on for odd people, who gave her pence
in return, with which she helped towards the housekeeping expenses. Moreover, poor little Betsy's
clothes were, many of them, past mending, and it was
strange indeed with some of them that one part held
by another. But Sarah Jones, the stonecutter's
daughter, a tidy lass and thrifty too in her way, and
belonging to well-to-do parents, never considered all
the trials of Betsy's lot, and was not slow to call her
" Odds and Ends," and " Rags and Tags," and " Miss
Coming-to-Pieces," and other descriptive names,
which Betsy neither coveted nor loved. The consequence was that these two, Betsy and Sarah
Jones, generally met in better humour than they
parted.

It was very cold when Betsy started for market,
and she thought of the poor little baby, and fancied
she felt it shiver, and remembered how it had had
bronchitis in the autumn, and so she took off mother's

shawl, which was round her own shoulders, and wrapped the baby well in it, and stopped at the corner of the street and asked the woman who kept the apple-stall to tie it round her and the baby together. When this was done, Betsy went on her way with satisfaction, and the baby, having only its round bald head exposed, snoodled down in the warm woollen wrap, evidently feeling as cosy as a cat when it sits and purrs on the rug before the fire and hears the kettle singing. The market was only just opened for the day, and but few customers arrived early, so Betsy was soon served with the little scraps of meat and the few vegetables that were all she had come to buy, and then, still cuddling up the baby close and tight, she turned to go home, and there, just beyond the market, was Sarah Jones.

"Good morning, Sarah," said Betsy, going up to her. "Is there any news?" Sarah Jones looked neat and tidy, and in her arms she carried her youngest brother, a pale little fellow, who sucked his thumb while his legs hung naked in the cold morning air.

"I have no time to trouble about news, Betsy," answered Sarah. "Mrs. Blake, next door to us, is ill, and there's plenty to do in thinking about her,

"WELL, LOOK AT YOUR BABY'S LEGS," SAID BETSY.—P. 81.

and then there's the wild beast show coming next
week. I've no time to think about news."

" Is there now, really? Well, if it's going to be
on a Saturday afternoon, I'll get mother to mind the
little ones and I'll go and see it."

" If I were you, Betsy," said Sarah Jones, " I'd
be careful how I carried that baby. You have got
it huddled up so, it won't know its legs from its arms
soon."

" It's not particular," said Betsy, " as long as it
knows they are there all safe." · Then Sarah Jones
looked at Betsy well from top to toe.

" Well, I must say," she exclaimed, " I wonder
you like to let people see you come out like that,
Betsy. Look at your arms and shoulders, nothing
on them, and a bitter day like this."

" Well, look at your baby's legs," said Betsy;
" there's nothing on them."

" Legs are not arms and shoulders, Betsy. I
shouldn't think of coming out without my jacket,
and I wonder you like to do· it."

" I haven't got a jacket," said poor little Betsy,
" and I took off mother's shawl to put round the
baby."

" Well, at any rate, you might mend up your

G

clothes a bit, Betsy," said Sarah Jones scornfully, as she turned to go on her way.

"Maybe I might," said Betsy, "and maybe you might do many things you don't do. I have my hands full, Sarah, and plenty to think of besides myself."

"I can always keep my things mended," said Sarah.

"You have time enough to do it in," cried Betsy, "and yet there's a slit in your apron, and maybe your nice warm jacket covers holes where I've no jacket to hide them. And yet though you can cover up yourself you can't cover up your baby. I'll tell you what it is, Sarah Jones," Betsy called after her, "if you thought less of yourself and more of your baby's legs it would be better for you."

Then Sarah Jones went home and put the baby on the floor, and took up her book and read for an hour or two, and was all the happier for knowing a little more to-day than she did yesterday, and the baby sneezed and coughed, and the next day it sneezed and coughed a little more, and in a week it had inflammation of the lungs, and every one said, "Dear me! poor little fellow!"

And Betsy went home, and her mother went out,

and Betsy scrubbed the floor, and cleaned all the things, and took care of the children, and thought of the wild beast show. The baby was well and warm enough, and sang a little song to itself that no-body else understood, and at the end of the day untidy little Betsy, forgetting to mend her rags, sat down and thought of Sarah Jones, and said to herself, " She's a nasty cat, and I can't bear her, and I never shall like good people who give themselves airs."

Now the moral of this story is what you please, but I think it is, " It's well to be neat and tidy, but it's still better to take care of the baby's legs."

THE IMITATION FISH.

It lived with three or four imitation ducks in a cardboard box, to which there was a glass lid. It was about an inch and a half long, and made of tin ; one side was painted a bright red, and the other a deep yellow. At the end of its nose was a very little bit of wire, and this bit of wire sadly puzzled the poor imitation fish. The ducks and the fish were all packed in soft cotton-wool, and placed in a quiet corner of the toy-shop.

The fish would have had a comfortable sleepy time if its nose had not been always longing to touch a strange little stick at the other end of the box. The ducks had no such longing and aching, at which the fish wondered much, until it noticed that they had no tiny bit of wire at the end of their noses, and somehow it could not help connecting this fact with their placid peacefulness.

One day, the ducks and fish and the little stick (which, with the exception of about a third of an inch

A FAIR LITTLE CHILD WITH GOLDEN HAIR.—P. 85.

at one end, was painted a bright red) were all violently
disturbed, and the next minute the lid of the box, in
which they had slept so long, was quickly pulled
open, and a fair little child with golden hair and
large grave blue eyes stood looking at them.

"Oh, you pretty ducks!" he cried, in a voice so
sweet that the imitation fish longed for a heart to
beat at its sound. "Oh, you pretty ducks, and you
dear little fish, I will take you home, and you shall
swim in the nice cool water." And the lid was
gently closed, and the child carried the box home to
a tall house by the sea. "Now you shall have a large
bath to swim in," the child said, "and you shall be
as happy as the day is long."

And then the gay little ducks and the red-and-
yellow fish were placed in the cool clear water, and
bravely swam upon its surface. Ah, how happy
they were, going round and round as the fancy of the
child directed, listening to the gleeful voice, and
sometimes feeling themselves taken up by the careful
fingers, looked at for a moment, and then tenderly
placed on the water again !

"Mother," the child asked, "what is the little
stick for ?"

"It is a magnet," the mother answered. And

then she showed the child how to hold it close to the little bit of wire at the end of the fish's nose, and lo! in a moment, the whole of the imitation fish's being seemed satisfied, and it clung to the stick as if the gift of life were in it, or swam swiftly and recklessly after it, as if a whirlwind were behind.

"There is only one fish, mother," the child said presently, taking the stick out of the water, "but there are three or four ducks. Poor little fish! how lonely you must be, with no other——"

Then a voice was heard calling, and the child vanished, leaving the fish and the ducks aimlessly waiting in the bath. Presently the mother came, and lifted them all out, and put them once more into their box.

"The dear child!" she said lovingly to herself; "all things are real to him as yet; even this foolish bit of painted tin he does not dream to be without life or feeling, for he knows nothing of things that are false."

And she placed the box on a shelf, and left the fish wondering greatly at the words it had heard.

The next morning the ducks and the little fish again swam about the bath, and chased the strange stick round and round, while the child laughed with

"DO ALL FISH LIVE IN THE SEA?"—P. 87.

glee, and was happy ; but the fish was not so bright as yesterday, for it remembered the words it had heard, and wondered much. And yet the child loved the little fish far more than the placid and contented ducks that troubled themselves not at all about anything.

"Don't be lonely, little fish," the dear voice would say, while the tender fingers put it away in the cotton-wool. "I will come and see you again to-morrow."

One day the little fish heard the child ask—

"Do all fish live in the sea, mother—in the great sea which is before our windows ?"

"All real fish do, my darling," the mother answered.

"And when they are taken out, mother, what then ?"

"They die—the real fish do."

And the poor imitation fish feared lest its falseness should be betrayed to the one heart that, knowing no falseness, thought it must be real ; but the mother said nothing more. And many times that day it was taken from its resting-place, and looked at long and lovingly, and kissed. And once the soft voice said—

"Ah, dear fish ! you shall not be lonely long. I

will not let you die, because I love you ; to-morrow
I will take you back to your great home, the sea."

Then the little fish, having learned to love the
child, trembled, for how could it bear to leave the one
thing that cared for it ?

And when the morrow came, the child took the
fish once more from its soft little home, and looked
at it for a few minutes with sorrowful blue eyes, and
then gently carried it away — away from the stick
and the imitation ducks and the little cardboard box
in which it had lived so long, and out of the house
by the sea, which was the child's home.

The sound of the waves came nearer and nearer,
and on and on the child went, until at last he stopped
at the end of a long pier, beneath which the water
rushed and foamed.   Then the child looked at the
imitation fish again, and kissed it for the last time,
while his tears fell upon its red-and-yellow sides.

"Farewell, dear little fish," he said.   "You shall
never be lonely more, or live in a stupid little cardboard box ; you shall go back to your home in the
sea, and dwell among others like you.   I love you,
dear little fish—farewell!" and the child dropped it
into the deep water beneath.   For one moment the
poor little imitation fish dimly saw out of one painted

eye the sweet face above, and then the waves tossed it away and away, farther and farther out to sea.

"Ah, dear child," it cried in terrible fear, "your purity has been the ruin of my false self. I was not made for things that were real; now I am indeed lost."

But no one took any notice of the poor toy, and the living fish swam past it with scarcely a glance; even they knew it was a sham; and when the fisherman cast his line into the sea, the hook at the end did not touch or hurt the imitation fish; all around it was heedless of its presence, only the waves went on tossing it day after day, week after week. Sometimes the sunlight came, and the real fish swam about and were glad; or the storms, and they crowded into the fisherman's net; but nothing pleased or hurt or harmed the imitation fish—only the waves went on tossing and tossing.

At last, after a long, long time, the waves seemed to be going on and on, always in one direction, and the fish went with them, until at last it was thrown on the shore among the pebbles and seaweed, and the little pools of water that collected between great stones; and the little fish was thankful, for it had escaped from a great loneliness, and the quiet of the

shore seemed a blessed thing after the ceaseless tossing of the waves.

How long it lay there it never knew, but one day
there was a sudden sound of a voice, and the little
fish was lifted up by hands almost as tender as the
child's.

"It is so like a toy my darling loved!" a voice
said; and a great happiness stole over the poor little
fish, for he knew the voice of the child's mother.
"He had a little fish that pleased him more than all
his other toys, but he thought it was real, and threw
it into the sea to make it happy," and she raised it to
her lips, and kissed it passionately again and again,
and bathed it in her tears. Then the little fish was
sad, and yet thankful and glad to feel itself gcing
back to the child.

And the mother put it in a soft hiding-place,
and looked at it many a time, kissing it tenderly;
for the sound of the child's voice was hushed, and
the blue eyes that had so lovingly watched the
imitation fish watched it never again — grave blue
eyes that were closed for evermore.

I'LL SING A SONG OF SUMMER-TIME.— P. 91.

BUTTERCUP QUEEN.

I'LL sing a song of summer-time,
  And crown my blue-eyed queen,
The prettiest queen the buttercups
  And I have ever seen.
Now gather up your pinafore,
  And scamper o'er the grass;
The daisies ne'er looked up to see
  A happier lad and lass.

We'll build a throne upon the sand,
  A mist is out at sea;
Perhaps beyond there is a land
  ⋅ Fresh made for you and me.
If you are true and I am true,
  We'll have no doubts and fears;
But laugh together all our lives,
  And live a thousand years.

Then let us sail away, my sweet,
    Before your crown shall fade;
For lovers true, like me and you,
    The summer-time was made.
Though buttercups can fade, my sweet,
    And summer-time can pass,
Yet just to-day we'll sail away,
    A happy lad and lass.

WE'LL BUILD A THRONE UPON THE SAND.—P. 92.

THE BEAUTIFUL LADY

THE woods were all white with the blossom of April and green with the coming of May. The larks were flying higher and higher watching for the swallows afar off—surely it was time they had started on their way?

The children went to the woods, but they were not singing for joy as usual; they followed the tall girl down the pathway.

" Janet," the little one said, " see, that is where the rabbit-holes used to be "; but Janet only nodded, and did not turn her head. " We never saw the rabbits," the little one added. " Do you think the lad ever saw them ?"

" I don't know," the tall girl answered; " but I think he would have told me if he had."

They filled their baskets with flowers and went out of the wood, and sauntered along the lane that led to the village.

" Janet," the little one asked, as they passed two

cottages that had been built just the year before, " is
it there the crazy woman lives?" One of the boys
laughed. "She's such a funny mad woman." But
before he could say more Janet turned round quickly.

"It is only a bad heart that laughs," she said; and
the boy was ashamed in a moment. "Come," she
added, "let us cover her window-ledge with flowers."
And eagerly the children stopped and piled up the
flowers on the window-sill, and then they tapped at
the window-pane.

"The fairies have been," they cried; "see what they
have left you;" and went on their way. They heard
the window opened and the woman's voice singing :—

> "And oh, my heart is sad to-day,
>   And oh, 'tis full of sorrow,
> For sweet my love is far away,
>   And won't be home to-morrow.
> And won't be home to-morrow-day,
>   And won't be home——"

Then she stopped with a little cry of joy, and the
children knew she had found the flowers.

The tall girl's heart gave a leap when she heard
the woman's cry, and she clasped the little one's hand
more tightly. "Ah, poor dear!" she thought, "the
lad at the carpenter's would have known how to comfort you with his talk of the strange lands your son's

eyes never saw, and the lad knew only in his heart."

All down the lane the children went—past the lilac-trees just bursting into bloom, past the farm-house,—they could hear the grunting of the pigs, and the rattle of the milking-pans the dairy-maid was washing as they passed by,—and on towards the village. But when they came in sight of their mother's cottage they stopped suddenly, for there, waiting by the door, stood a grand carriage.

" Janet," they whispered, afraid to speak aloud, "it must be the beautiful lady." They stood still, not liking to go on and wondering what to do. But the little one looked up and said—

" I do want to see the beautiful lady." So they gathered courage and went slowly on to the cottage, and one by one they shyly entered in at the door, curtseying as they did so, for the beautiful lady sat by the fireplace talking to the mother. The little one was glad the china dog she won off the Christmas-tree stood upon the mantelpiece, for half a dozen times did the beautiful lady look up at it; and for ever afterwards it seemed to have a remembrance of her, though it only told it to the little one.

Janet had learnt all manner of things from the carpenter's lad—to love books and the histories of far-off lands, and all manner of strange stories ; and in the evening she talked to the children of all she knew. So when they saw the beautiful lady they thought of the fairy-queen who loved a mortal man and took him off to fairyland, and they fell to wondering if this could be she. She had blue eyes and soft golden hair, which was twisted all round her head, till it looked just like a crown. She had surely listened while Thomas the Rhymer played upon his harp, they thought ; and perchance she knew where the three roads met and one branched off to Elfinland. She had taken her gloves off, and they saw that on her little finger she wore a gold ring with a green stone set in it. Perhaps when she was tired of earth, they thought, she turned it round three times and found herself in fairyland once more. And while they thought all this, and stood in a group staring at her, they heard the clicking of the harness on the horses, and knew that really she was no fairy at all, but just the beautiful lady who had come to live in the big house beyond the bridge ; but of course she might have been the fairy-queen—it seemed so odd that she was not. She turned and looked at the

children with her sweet blue eyes, and then she said
—it seemed a wonderful thing to hear her voice—

" I have come to ask your mother about a boy
who lived in this village. He was a cobbler's son;
I know his sister." Then all speaking together the
children answered—

" The strange lad at the carpenter's."

" Did you know him?" the lady asked.

" Yes, we all knew him," they answered, "but
Janet knew him best. He used to take us to the
woods to show us the rabbit-holes. They are not
there now, and we never saw the rabbits. He used
to tell us stories about the strange countries, and of
all the things he meant to do."

" And while he was thinking of all the great ends
he would gain he forgot to make any beginning," the
mother said. She was a stern woman, but her voice
was sad while she spoke. " He was always dreaming," she added, "and while he was dreaming his
hands were folded."

Then the beautiful lady sighed but made no answer,
for she thought how many of us are like the cobbler's
son, longing to climb great heights, looking up at the
far-off light, yet standing still the while; and as for
the things we see and do in dreams,—should we not

H

most of us travel far and wide and achieve great things indeed, if we could but tack our hands and feet on to our fancies?

The tall girl who had known the boy so well, went forward a step.

"He worked hard all day," she said gently; "he did all that was given him to do. It was only in the evening that he read books and thought of the strange countries and told us of his dreams and of all he meant to do. Once he made a little table," she began, but before she could say more the beautiful lady interrupted her.

"I know," she said, "it is in my brother's home far away in India. It was my mother's, and because it was made so well she once sent it down to the schoolhouse, so that all the village boys might see it, and know how well a cobbler's little son could work."

"Yes, yes," the children cried, eagerly crowding up close round the beautiful lady; "oh, go on and tell us more, we know he made a little table."

"And as it was coming back from the schoolhouse," she went on, "the man who carried it let it fall, and a little piece of wood that was not so firmly glued as the rest fell from the under part, and we saw that beneath it had been written: '*Daddy's lad made this table, and sent it into the world with his love,*' and we all thought much about these words, and how the cobbler's little son had put one thing at least that was well done into the world. And when my brother went away to India, he asked my mother for the little table, and he took it with him; and in one of his letters he said it always seemed to him more like a living thing with a human voice than a bit of furniture."

"He was a clever lad," the mother sighed, her stern face relaxing a little.

"He used to tell us about all manner of things," the children said; "we were never tired of hearing."

"But it was all waste of time," the mother said.

"No, dear mother," the tall girl answered gently, "I do not think so, for we all loved him, and somehow after he came we all loved each other more." Then the mother's eyes suddenly filled with tears.

"His heart was stronger than his hands," she said to the beautiful lady, "and what the girl says is true; he taught us to love better, but he never knew it. And he loved the children, and the birds, and the bats, and the bees, and the sunshine, and the flowers that grew in the woods. It was wonderful how he loved them all."

"And they loved him back again!" the tall girl said, eagerly.

Then the beautiful lady gently touched the mother's arm that was brown and bare, and said softly—

"He did not only dream, dear woman, and there are some dreams far better and sweeter than any waking."

"But the pity of it is that we live our lives awake," the woman said. "But the poor lad," she added sadly, "he sleeps on just by the pathway between the church and the schoolhouse."

"Come and see," the little one cried, "oh, dear beautiful lady, come and see!" and almost before she knew it, the beautiful lady had risen from her seat and taken the little one by the hand and left the cottage; the tall girl walked by her side, and the children followed in a group. So they went on to the place where the carpenter's lad slept well.

It was close by the pathway, just as the mother had said, so that if he did not sleep too soundly, he could hear the children's voices singing in the school-house, or the patter-patter of their feet when the church clock struck the hour, at which the schoolhouse door opened wide, and they came joyfully forth and hurried away to their homes.

"He is here," said the children softly, and they stood still, while the beautiful lady looked down at the grass growing wild and tall above him.

"We told the man not to cut the grass often," they whispered; "for when it grows up high it seems like the woods, and he was always so happy in the woods."

"There are some wildflowers growing among the grass," the beautiful lady said.

"Ah, yes," the tall girl answered, "we don't know how it is, but there are always flowers among the grass above him; we think sometimes that perhaps they are his little dreams coming through."

THE STORY OF WILLIE AND FANCY.

I.

IT always seemed to Willie as if other children knew so many more things than he did, as if they played at some game at which he was left out, as if they had some clue to life and its enjoyment which he had somehow missed. Perhaps it was only because he had never known any children of his own age. His father and mother were dead, and he lived with his grandparents in a little cottage at the top of the hill, just about a mile from the village. There were two other cottages adjoining his grandfather's, but no one had lived in them since he could remember, and all three cottages were nearly tumbling down and yet never quite tumbled. The grandfather used to say it was a bad thing to live in a broken-to-bits cottage, but he never thought of leaving it. Willie was left to do just as he liked, for his grandparents were very old, and did not know how to amuse a little boy. His grandmother, to be sure, cut up her husband's old clothes for him, and made him a seed-cake once a fortnight, but that was all. The cut-up clothes were very funny ; the trousers were generally too short, and the jacket sleeves too long, and the pockets were never in the right place; but somehow they always seemed to go well with Willie's grave little face, and large blue eyes, and soft hair, that was brown in the shade and gold in the sun.

He was very lonely in the winter-time, for his grandmother was very old and nervous, and did not like his wandering about in the cold or when the snow was on the ground.

"You might fall and break your leg," she said; "and then what would you do ? Wooden legs are dear to buy and awkward to walk with; besides boots are always bought in pairs, and one boot would be wasted if you had no foot to put it on, so it is real economy to stay at home and keep two legs, my dear!" And Willie looked up with his big blue eyes at his grandmother, and said—

"Yes, granny, dear; but the odd boots would do to throw at the sparrows in the cherry-tree."

"It would never do to throw new boots at them," his grandmother answered; "it would frighten the poor little sparrows, for they have been used to old ones so long."

And so all through the winter Willie seldom went far from the cottage; but he amused himself by getting over the fence into the next-door gardens, and then by the unbolted doors into the empty cottages. He was never tired of going through and through the deserted rooms. He looked in all the empty cupboards, and stood before all the rusty little fireplaces, trying to imagine what the people, who had dwelt there once, had been like; the people who had lived, and laughed, and worked, and wept, between the mouldy grimy walls; who had sat over the damp fireplaces, and kept their good things in the bare cupboards, and who had died or journeyed on to other places.

"Perhaps there were children," he thought once, "and perhaps they ran in and out, and sang, and danced, and gathered the fruit in the garden in the summer, and played at snowball in the winter. I would give the world to have seen them."

In the summer-time he was not nearly so lonely, for then he could go off for the whole day if he pleased, and wander about in the fields and woods, or over the brow of the hill to look at the long straight

A LITTLE GROUP OF CHILDREN ROUND THE DOOR OF THE FORGE.—P. 105.

road beyond,—he never knew where that road led to,—and in the evening he went home past the black-smith's shop. The blacksmith lived just half-way between the village and the cottage, and there was generally a little group of children round the door of the forge; and Willie used to stand too, and watch the sparks fly upwards, and listen to the sound of the blacksmith's hammer; but he always stood a little way off from the others, for they were strange to him, and he was shy. The blacksmith's little daughter was generally sitting by the door sewing; it seemed as if she stitched away at the same piece of blue-checked linen for ever. She was evidently making something, but Willie often thought it had had no beginning and would have no end, that for ever the blacksmith would be hammering at his anvil, and for ever his little daughter would be sitting by the door, stitching away at the same piece of coarse blue linen.

"Grandfather," Willie asked one day, "is it far to the rest of the world?"

"The rest of the world?" his grandfather said looking up; "why, what are you thinking of, lad?"

"I want to see it, that is all; is it far?"

"It depends what part you want to see, it's a long way from end to end of the world, if that is what you mean; and a vast deal lies between."

"Shall I ever see it all, grandfather?"

"No, I should say not. I have seen little enough myself, and I don't know how you are going to see more. By and by you'll have to learn, and when you have done learning you'll have to work, and when you have done working, and maybe before, you'll have to die. That's what life is for most of us, lad—one after another, one after another; little enough difference there is in the lives of us, take them all round."

"But some work in one way and some in another," the old man's wife said, looking up quickly; "and it's the business of some to travel far, and of some to stay at home."

"Tell me more, granny dear," the boy said eagerly. His grandmother thought about more things than his grandfather did, or at any rate talked about more, and Willie liked best to listen to her. "What does one do if one wants to travel?"

"Get ready—ready for what one means to do."

"Get what ready, dear granny?"

The old woman took her knitting, put on her

glasses, and looking up into her little grandson's face, said quickly, "Oneself."

He waited a minute and then he asked, "What shall I be when I am a man, dear granny?"

"How can I tell, lad? you are only a boy yet. Bless me," she said suddenly, "but you are eight years old, and it is time you took to getting ready to be a man." Then she turned to her husband. "Tom, the boy is eight years old. We must write to the city and ask John what we shall do with him." The old woman's eldest son, who was a lawyer, lived in the city. He was a clever man, who had taught himself nearly all he knew and had made money, for people were glad to get his advice. "Yes, we must write to John. He will tell us what to do with the lad. What would you like to be, Willie, some day when you are a man?"

Then Willie thought for a few minutes.

"Granny, dear, I should like to be something that should take me right to the end of the world; I want to see what there is there. And I should like to go to sea in a ship and to be wrecked; oh, granny, I should like it so; and to escape in a little boat while the waves tossed and tossed all about, and we rode over them and over them ever so high."

The old woman laid down her knitting, and took off her spectacles and wiped them well, and put them on again. "Willie, my little lad," she said, "you have been reading books. Now, where did you get them?"

"It's only the book up on grandfather's shelf, grandmother. I looked at the picture, and then I thought I should like to be one of the people in the boat."

"Ah, well, people are safe enough once they are in a picture, but no one knows what they have had to go through before they got there. Don't let pictures unsettle your mind, lad, and set you hankering after dangerous things that do you no good till they are past and gone, and maybe have taken you with them."

"Oh, grandmother, but I am tired of seeing so little and being so little; I want to see more."

"Ah, it's wonderful the things one wants and never gets. It takes a long time to understand how little it is one ever gets of what one wants," the grandfather said. "One grows used to doing without at last and so content."

"More's the pity if one's young," the old woman answered; and then she turned to Willie again and said, "Learn to do without things, lad; but never to

be content not to get them while you have hands to
work, and feet to run, and a head to think. Try
after all things; but not to keep them, for they are
better worth winning for others than for oneself.
Remember that, dear, as long as you live."

"But I don't know any one to do things for,
except you and grandfather," the boy said, puzzled.
He often wondered how it was that his grandmother
talked so strangely. After the first few minutes she
sometimes said things that seemed to belong not to
the old woman who lived in the cottage and knitted
day in and day out, and who thought of nothing save
the chickens and the cherry-tree and the making of
cakes and clothes for Willie and the keeping of the
cottage tidy, but to some past life, and to some world
in which she lived no longer, and of whose ways some
knowledge lingered unknown to her memory; it was
almost as if some past self awoke, a self of which
the present one was unconscious.

"I don't know any one but you and grandfather
to do things for, and even then I don't know how to
do them, or how to begin, granny dear."

"You won't have far to look. There'll be a
crowd waiting when you lift up your eyes, dear.
One has never far to seek when one has a mind to

help—learn how to do first, and the chance to do will be at your elbow."

"Ah, but, grandmother, I want to see so much, and first of all, I want to go right to the end of the world."

"Well, well," she said, and took up her knitting again, "we'll ask your uncle John. There's little that he cannot give one advice about. Your grandfather shall write soon enough. Go out and see that the chickens are gone to roost, and take a little run over the brow, and maybe you'll think less of the end of the world for to-night."

Then Willie went out and looked at the chickens. They fluttered their wings and flew past him as he entered the fowl-house, for they were just settling down to roost and did not want to be disturbed. He pulled-to the door of the fowl-house, and then he went out at the little wooden gate by the side of the cottage, and ran along the road that led over the hill. "If I could only run to the end of the world," he thought, "or to the great sea, and hear the waves. I don't want to do things," he went on. "I want to see them."

There was a little grassy bank at the side of the road; he sat down to think, and rested his face in

his hand so long, wondering and wondering, that he
did not notice the twilight gather closer and closer
around him, or the mist rise up from the river and
the fields, and wrap the trees in a soft gray cloak
and hide all things before him. It was odd, but as
he sat there, it seemed as if he could hear a soft voice
singing the words that were running in his head—

" Right to the end of the world, my dear ;
   Right to the end of the world." ·

" It isn't a song," he said to himself. " It is only
what I was saying to myself, and yet I thought I
heard some one else singing it." He looked up; but
there was no one near. He saw the mist then. He
felt it softly touching his face and hair. It made
him think of the waves and the sailors. " If I could
but see them just once," he cried.

" I will take you, Willie ; come with me," he
heard a voice say ; and, looking up quickly, he saw
that on the dewy green bank beside him a little
girl was sitting. He looked at her face long and
gravely. He could see it well in the dim light. It
was very beautiful, and he had never seen it before;
but yet he felt that he and she knew each other.
He remembered her as one remembers some sweet
dream, forgetting when one dreamt it. She had soft

restless eyes that seemed to have a thousand things to say; her hair was like threads of gold, and fell down to her waist, and her mouth was sweet, and her smile was bright. Oh, she was lovely, and never was any one half so sweet as Fancy when Willie first saw her.

"Dear Fancy," he said, for he knew her name quite well, "have you come to me?" Then she crept up closer to him.

"We will go so far together," she said softly. "Oh, Willie, you are not afraid, are you? The sea is creeping up to us. It has overtaken the river. It is sweeping over the meadows. Are you afraid?" she whispered. Then he held her tight and close, and her face was pale, and he saw no longer the gold upon her hair or the sweetness in her eyes, for the night had grown dark and the wind had risen and cried out shrilly from tree to tree, and slowly and surely the great sea was coming with many a leap and many a roar over the meadows and over the hill towards them. And yet he knew that somewhere, afar off in some still corner that fled back and back as the sea came on, the cottage was safe; the danger was only for him and for Fancy, and he was brave for both. And still the waves came madly on till suddenly they were at his feet, and then he ran, holding Fancy close, so that no harm should come to her.

"Perhaps we could ride on the waves," she whispered. "See, there is a great ship; the wind is driving it on. Oh, we are going already; hold my hand; hold fast, lest we be lost." But he could hear no more, for they were riding on and on, over and over the great waves, faster and faster than the ship, and nowhere was anything to be seen save the blackness and the sea and the sky and the great ship being driven on. Soon they overtook the ship. They saw the man at the wheel. They knew that he was not thinking of the storm and the waves, but of a little cottage high up upon a cliff, and of the sunshine falling down upon it, and of a woman shading her eyes with her hands and for ever turning her face southwards and watching, while the children played among the flowers and asked, "When will he come home, dear mother? when will he come home?" On went Willie and Fancy, on and on. There was a little boat, tossing higher and higher while Death rode on in front, but, oh so slowly! Willie could have cried out with fear, for he knew the boat would overtake it, and he saw the wild eyes

I

and the scared white faces of the wrecked as they with their last hope passed by. On went Willie and Fancy, on and on, till far above them shone one little star, and the water became suddenly smooth, and the waves rocked them as a mother rocks her child to sleep, and gently carried them home to the cottage-gate, and in a minute Fancy had waved her hand to him, and Willie had climbed the narrow stairs that led to the little room in which he slept.

He heard Fancy's voice long after she had left him. He heard it in his dreams that night. "We will go so far," she whispered. "We will see the end of the world together."

II.

"WHERE shall we go?" Fancy asked; "where shall we go to-day? The sun is in the sky, the flowers are all in bloom, and the birds are singing. Where shall we go to-day?" She did not wait for an answer, but danced all down the wood, taking the strangest flights and singing the wildest songs, telling Willie a hundred things he had never heard before, teaching him to hear where till now he had heard no sound, and to see where formerly he' had seen nothing. He never knew how they went, how high they climbed, or the names of the places he passed, or of the people he met, but none of them were strange to him, for Fancy knew them well, and made them all known to him.

"Dear Fancy," he said, "why did you not come before? I have been alone so long; till you came I had no companion."

"You did not call me," she cried. "You did not want me till the days when you went through and through the empty cottages thinking of all the people who once dwelt there; and then, though you said no word, I heard your voice calling me faintly, and I came a little nearer and a little nearer until at last I was sitting by you on the grassy bank."

"And when shall we go to the end of the world?" he asked. "Let it be soon, for I am always thinking of it."

"We will go to-night," she said, "this very night. I will tap at the window-pane when you have slept one single hour, and then you must wake up and open wide the window, and there on the window-ledge I will be waiting."

"How shall we get down?"

"We will climb down by the cherry-tree, and soon we will be far away."

"Is it very far?" he asked; "for what will grandmother say?"

"It is very far, but we shall soon be there;" and then Fancy skipped away.

He saw her at the end of the wood, the sun still shining on her hair, and he held out his hands and called, "Come back for a little while now, and sing me one song more, dear Fancy;" but she laughed a merry mocking laugh, and was gone.

"Where have you been, my little lad?" his grandmother asked, "and what have you been doing?"

"Oh, grandmother," he said, "I am so happy. I shall never be lonely more;" but his grandmother had no desire to listen.

"Ah, well, you will have to go to school soon and learn, and then you'll have less time on your hands," was all she said.

"Am I to go to school?" he asked.

"Your grandfather has written to uncle John about it. The blacksmith's little daughter is going to school, and she is younger than you. She is going to learn some day how to teach others. It is time you were thinking of your books too." And then the grandmother took up her knitting. "A great man is your uncle John," she said presently, "a very great man; and all his greatness is his own doing. We never thought he'd be the man he is." Then suddenly she said, "There's a large cake in the oven, dear lad; do you think you could go and turn it?"

So Willie went and turned the cake, and then sat down on the rug and looked at the great tabby cat fast asleep, and listened to the ticking of the clock, and thought how much he longed to see all the world before he did any work in it; and then he smelt the cake, and remembered how kind his grandmother was to him. While he had been wandering away with Fancy, she had been making that good cake for him to eat, and working for him; yet here was he, who had never done anything in the world, grumbling and discontented because some day he would have to make a beginning. He got up and went back to his grandmother, and put his arms round her neck and his little face close to hers.

"Dear granny," he said, "I will be a great man some day if I can. I will try to be like uncle John. Perhaps Fancy will teach me."

"Fancy! Fancy will teach you nothing," she said. "Don't waste your time on Fancy;" and then she looked into the little lad's blue eyes and grave pale face. "It is by your own head and your own heart that you will be great, my dear, if you have the will to mind them."

III.

"WILLIE, Willie," called Fancy, "are you ready? I am waiting;" and in a minute Willie sprang up and opened the window; he was dressed, and had been listening for her tap. He clambered on to the window-ledge, and then together they jumped into the cherry-tree and down to the garden beneath. He stopped for a moment and looked round—at the cottage, and his own little window wide open, and the fowl-house, and the empty cottages beyond, and at the cherry-tree above him, and at Fancy—Fancy with her golden hair and restless eyes and eager bright face beside him.

"Are we going to the end of the world?" he asked with a sigh, for he had longed so much for this strange journey.

"Yes, we are going," answered Fancy; "are you ready?"

"Yes, I am ready; but wait a minute," he said, and picked a rose. It fell to pieces as he held it, and the rose leaves fluttered to his feet. He looked down at it, and something like a sob was in his throat, though he did not know why. It is long years since that summer night, and he has travelled far, and seen much, and many things are known to him now, yet no memory of past days stays with him more faithfully or is sweeter than the memory of this one evening when he stood beneath the cherry-tree with Fancy by his side and the rose leaves at his feet, waiting to start for the end of the world, he and Fancy hand in hand together.

"Come," said Fancy, "come;" and, looking into her eyes, and giving himself up to her guidance, they started. Slowly down the garden they went, over the fence at the bottom, then quickly across the field. They passed the blacksmith's cottage; there was a light in the window, for the blacksmith's wife was stitching at new clothes for her little daughter. On through the village they went; they heard the neighbours talking in the doorways, but they did not stay to listen. "We must run," said Fancy. "Hold my hand tighter;" and through the woods and along the roads and over the great high hills, faster and faster they ran; they saw the twinkling lights of the city, and in a minute they were there; they heard a mother weeping, for her little one had died; they heard some merrymakers singing till the voices grew faint in the distance. "Quicker, quicker," cried Fancy, "for we must journey faster than the wind and faster than time, and as yet we have not overtaken the middle of the night; the city is not sleeping yet: faster—faster—faster!" she cried, and on they went beyond the city and over the moors. They saw the mountains in the distance; the moon was slowly climbing them. On and on through the dense forests; on and on through the villages, and over the shining waters, past great cities, with their high buildings and their towers and their steeples; past the scattered houses around and beyond them—the houses that seemed as if they would have crept into the throng had their courage been great enough; past every habitation in which man could live, on and on, faster and faster went Willie and Fancy, till fewer and fewer became the landmarks, and farther and farther apart all things that the hand of man had placed, and taller and thicker were the trees, and vaster and vaster the great bare tracks of land, and then at last amid mighty stones that seemed hurled from some unseen height,—mountains and forest and sea and cities all far behind; then at last Willie and Fancy stood at the end of the world. Before them were only the clouds and the great moon shining, and the little stars that seemed like golden stairs leading up higher and higher; and beyond and above all towered two mountains in the midst of the stars and the clouds; the one bathed in golden light; the other dark and drear, wild and rugged with strange masses of blackness clinging to it.

"Come up higher, come up higher," he could hear Fancy calling. "The little stars shall be your steps; come up higher." And with his eyes still straining upwards, he went on climbing, up and up, treading on the stars till they were far beneath his feet and even the moon was behind, until at last he halted and saw the world afar off beneath him.

"Fancy," he cried, "Fancy, where are you?"

"I am here beside you," she whispered, for she was half afraid.

"There is a woman up there; tell me what she is doing?" Then Fancy looked up and laughed a wild strange laugh; it almost made Willie shudder, it seemed so out of place.

"She is there to rub up the world," laughed Fancy. "Oh, it takes a great deal of rubbing, so many people make it dull, so few make it bright; and there she sits for ever working away, but it is little enough she can do, so little that few besides the children find the bright places."

"What are the two hills over there? why is one dark and one so bright?"

"They are the sunshine and the storms. The one is made of laughter and of gladness, of all the good that people do; the other of tears and sorrow and misery and vice; from the one the sunbeams and the warm sweet days of summer journey; from the other is hurled the storms, and from it steals the darkness. Every smile you cause, every good thing you do, makes the one hill taller, and is given back as sunshine into the world. Every tear you cause others to shed, every wrong you do, is heaped on to the dark hill there, and helps to make the sad days and stormy ones. Of joy and sorrow, of light and darkness, is the whole world made."

IV.

"GET up," called the grandmother; "it is the first day of school; get up, lad, and feed the chickens, and hurry away to the village."

"Oh, grandmother, but I like the woods so well," Willie answered.

"Uncle John says you are to learn, learn on until he comes in the spring, and then he will see what you are fit for." So Willie got up and fed the chickens, and took his books and went to school. He passed the blacksmith's shop, but the blacksmith's daughter was learning too, and no longer sat by the door of the forge. All down the road Fancy went by his side, singing tó him in the fresh sweet morning ; but he had no time to listen to her, he had to think of all he was going to do.

The first day and the first week and the first month went by, and every morning saw Willie going to the village ; at first Fancy always went by his side, but he found that her songs came between him and his books, and he turned his head away and would not hear her, and would not see her, until at last she troubled him no more.

The days were not so sweet when she had ceased to sing him songs, and to take him breathless journeys, and tell him of the strange things that were or that might be between the earth and sky. He went on day after day trying to do his best, making his happiness in seeing his grandmother's face light up when he was first in his class, or in hearing his grandfather say, "Ah, he's a good lad; he'll be as great as his

uncle John some day." At night, when he had learned
his lessons, he went to sleep quickly lest Fancy should
come and carry him off on some strange journey, and
so unfit him for the next day's work. Yet how he
sometimes thought of her, and longed for her, and
dreamt for a little while of those days that would
surely come, when he and she would once more be
companions!

At last the winter came; and with it the holidays; and Willie, being older, was allowed to walk
about as he pleased, and so he wandered through
the leafless woods, and over the brow of the hill,
and looked again and again at the long straight
road, wondering to what strange city it might
lead.

One day, when the snow was on the ground, he
went into the woods, and sat down beneath a tree, to
think a while. The few leaves that lingered were
sere and yellow, but as he looked down the pathway
he thought, as he shivered, that they would look like
gold, if the sun would but shine through the trees.
And as he thought this, suddenly he looked up, and
there was Fancy. But, ah! how she was changed!
All the colour had gone from her face, her eyes were
sad, her hair was dull.

"Fancy," he said, "is it you?" and his heart smote him for forgetting her.

"Yes, it is I," she answered, sadly and bitterly.

"But how you are changed!" he said. "The blue is gone from your eyes, and the gold from your hair. Oh, Fancy, you are not so bright as you used to be."

"How can I be?" she cried. "You will not hear me, you will not see me, you will not listen if I sing, or follow if I lead. How can I be the same?"

Then the tears came into Willie's eyes.

"Sing to me," he said; "sing one of your old sweet songs, dear Fancy, and let me wander with you again." Then Fancy tried to sing, but her voice was weak and faltering, and she broke down in the middle of her song and sobbed.

"Oh, I cannot, I cannot," she cried, "for I am starved."

"And I am almost frozen," said Willie, his teeth chattering with cold. "But come closer, Fancy, and tell me what I can do to help you. Oh, my sweet Fancy," he cried, "how happy we have been together!"

"But you are frozen," she said; "what is the use of you? Is your heart cold too?"

"Oh no," he answered, "that is very warm; it always is."

"Let me creep in there," she whispered, "and make it my home; and I will grow bright again, and make the world bright for you; and I will tell you strange stories, and sing you sweet songs, which you shall hear in your sleep, and call dreams. Take me into your heart, dear Willie, and let me rest there."

"Fancy, oh Fancy," he cried, "there is no one so sweet as you, even now;" and he held out his arms, and she nestled down in them, and found her home at last. For many a day was she there; many a lonely hour did she beguile for Willie; many a song she sang to him, and many a tale she told him; and sometimes, when he had worked hard and yet could not accomplish what he wished, she would whisper some sound to him, that helped him, he hardly knew how, to do what before he had given up as hopeless.

But the months went on, and Willie had so much to do that, though Fancy still stayed in his heart, he had no time to listen to her; and then sorrow came to him, for his grandfather died; and his heart was so full of grief there was no room in it for Fancy.

"I must work hard and learn all things, so that I may know how to comfort you, dear granny," he said; ".and by and by we will live together in the cottage again."

But she answered, " Oh no, dear lad, you will be great when you are a man, and the people will want you to go and live among them, to make their lives better."

And still Fancy stayed by his side, half hoping that one day he would turn from his work, and see her, and once again go journeying with her. She hád grown small and thin, and sad and grave, and her steps were slow and soft, and she was afraid to whisper to him lest he should tell her that the time for play had passed and the time for work had come, and send her from him.

At last there came the day on which she left him. Willie had grown tall and strong, and had to choose what he would be when he should be a man; and then his uncle sat down and talked to him of all the things that he might do. When Willie had listened, he looked up and said, " Uncle John, I should like to be a lawyer." And when Fancy heard that sad word she fled away from him swiftly and for ever.

She went back again to the cottage, and the woods, and the fields where she and Willie had been so happy, and sadly roamed alone, until the blacksmith's little daughter, dreaming over her poetry books one day, went fast asleep, and Fancy, stealing up to her, crept into her life and held fast to it for ever.

Long afterwards, when the blacksmith's little daughter had become a woman, and was a teacher of others, and lived in a schoolhouse, Willie met her and wondered why it was he found some new beauty in her face. In her eyes there seemed to be some strange history that was half his own, and he thought that life with her would be sweeter than any life without her.

At last he fell to wondering if she would marry him, so that he might have her with him always; and when she said " Yes," and everything around seemed changed and brighter far than it had since he had wandered away from the cherry-tree, he never for a moment thought that the reason was just this—that the blacksmith's daughter had taken his Fancy.

THE BOY WAS TURNING OVER THE LEAVES OF A BOOK.—P. 129.

IN THE PORCH.

I.

THEY sat down in the porch, the two women and the boy, and the stranger who had come from the country. The old woman was spinning, and the young one was sewing, and the stranger was watching the rain-clouds gather. The boy was turning over the leaves of a book in which the lives of great men were written down.

"I would give the world to know a great man," he said, and the spinner looked up and answered—

"Ah! it is a grand thing; one feels one knows the world when one knows a great man."

"And what is greatness?" asked the woman from the country; and then they were all silent, each wondering how the others would answer. And at last the boy spoke again, looking round at the women—

"Have any of you known a great man?" he

·K

asked, and again they were silent ; but presently the
spinner said—

"When I was young, there was a rich man living
in the town; he must have been great, for he was
very rich, and over his grave there stands a tall
marble monument."

"And what did he do?" asked the boy.

"I don't know what he did; but once when he
was young he had no money, so he set to work, and
he worked and worked hard, so that long before he
was middle-aged he became very rich; and then he
built a great house and lived in it, and kept grand
horses and carriages, and when he drove through the
town, all the people looked after him with wonder."

"But what good deeds did he do?" asked the boy,
"and what great things?"

"I never heard of any good deeds," the spinner
answered ; "he had no time to think of the poor, or
to fight battles as the heroes did ; but he worked
hard to' become rich, and he had all things that
money could buy."

"It is a good thing to work," said the woman
from the country.

"And was he learned?" asked the boy.

"Ah, I do not know," the spinner said. "He may

have been, but he had his business to think of, and
he did not talk much, or write books, or paint
pictures, or teach others; none can tell how much
he knew."

"And had he many friends ?"

"He had little time to make friends, and none
knew him well ; but sometimes rich men sat at his
table, and ate and drank, and invited him to their
houses, but he had little time to go, and little to say
when he went, for he had to think of all the ways of
making money, so that his riches might exceed those
of other men."

"And had he wife and children ?"

"Oh no," said the spinner, shaking her head
sadly ; "he had no time to give to his affections,
and his heart had no room for them."

"And for what did he work?"

"He worked to become rich, and to live among
the things that money buys, and so that, if he chose,
he might live at ease. He was a great man to win
all these things for himself."

"And who loved him ?"

"There were none who loved him, but some
feared him, and many longed to be as rich as he."

"And had he never lived, what then ?"

"Dear lad, I cannot tell: another would have been in his place, and the money that he earned would have been in other hands, but I cannot tell in whose."

"And what was the good of him?"

"I do not know. But he was a great man, and when he died, he left directions for a grand marble tomb."

"And what was the good of that?" asked the boy.

"Ah, lad, if our name is written in no human heart, and none care to remember it, and if there are no books and no deeds called after us, is it not a great thing to have it written up on marble? It would be sad indeed if there were no room anywhere on earth for it: there was room on a marble tomb for his."

"Did any weep for him?"

"No, there were none to weep for him; but the marble monument is there, tall and fine."

"Do any remember him?"

"Few remember him, and none care to think of him; but there are some distant cousins of his in a far-off land, and these spend his money: they had no need of it, and they never saw his face, but they spend his money with a lavish hand—all the gold and silver which he had heaped up. Oh, he was a great man, and very rich." And then the spinner was silent."

II.

"AND now tell me," said the boy, turning to the young woman, " did you ever know a great man ?"

" I have known so few people," she answered, thoughtfully. She was silent for a few minutes, and then spoke again. " When I was a little girl," she said, " there was a poor woman who lodged for a time in my mother's cottage. She was very poor; she had only a few clothes and a little shoe that her father, who was a cobbler, had left unfinished when he died, and she had an old sampler which she had worked when she was a child. One day she showed the little shoe to the village cobbler, and I think he always worked better afterwards ; for he said he had never seen work better done than the work that was in the unfinished shoe, and he felt ashamed of his own bad stitches. When the woman had been a year in my mother's house she died, and left my mother all she had, just the old clothes, and the little shoe, and the sampler. On the sampler there was worked the name and age of the worker, 'Sarah Short, aged 7 years,' and right down at the bottom there was written on the frame, 'I have tried to work this well, for Daddy said *good work lives on for ever.*' And my mother told me to take these words to heart, and then she hung the sampler up over the fireplace in our little sitting-room. And one day, just a few years ago, an artist came to my mother's cottage, and asked if he could lodge there for the summer while he painted a picture ; so we made room for him, and every day he went out to paint the view from the hillside. He was not strong when he came, and he was sorely disheartened about his work, for he was poor, and no one bought his pictures ; though he tried hard to paint his very best, no one seemed to care for them or to notice them. He was almost in despair when he came, and beginning to think that it was of no use working well, or hoping for good things to come. After a bit he lost patience with the picture he was painting, for it took so much time, and he was not sure that any would buy it, or that those who cared for pictures would ever see it, and so he put it away, and began painting portraits of the village folk. He painted many, and there was one delicate child whose little face he painted just for love of it; and because he loved the child he took so much pains with the portrait that he did it better than all the others, and those who saw it stood for a long time looking at the pale little face, and the large blue eyes; and then I think they fell to thinking of things far better than themselves. At last there were no more portraits to paint, and the painter seemed to lose all heart again, and he used to take a book and go to the woods and spend the whole day in reading. My mother was grieved for him, for she saw that he was poor, and that fame and money would be very sweet to him. One day "—the young woman stopped for a moment and looked up at the boy, scarcely seeing him, but thinking of the days that were gone, and living once more in them—"it seems like yesterday," she said with a sigh, and then went on— "one day when he was going out, and had to pass as usual through our little sitting-room, his eye caught the old sampler hanging up over the fireplace, and he went up to it and looked at it, and then he read the words beneath, *Good work lives on for ever.*' He read them and turned away, and then went back and read them again. The next morning he took the unfinished picture to the hillside again and worked at it with a will to which he had been a stranger many a day. He worked at it every day, oh, so carefully. Many a bit he painted out and painted in again, and many a night he was dissatisfied with his whole day's work, but still he went on and on. It seemed as if there was something in his heart that he painted right into the picture, and besides this, he painted all he saw, and at last when it was done, and one looked at it, one fancied one could hear the birds sing, and feel the sweet summer air coming from the south. I always thought when I saw it," continued the woman, "that it was a blessed thing for us all to live in so beautiful a world, and a sin and a sorrow when we did anything to disgrace it. There are few of us," she added, "who can do things worthy of it : that is too great a happiness for many of us to reach.

"At last the painter went away, and we heard no more of him for a long time, not till the next year, and then news came that every one was talking of his pictures—that they were hanging in the Exhibition, and were counted the best there—and the pictures were the view from the hillside and the portrait of the little child. And we were all so proud and happy in the village, thinking of the grand people

who would see our child's face and the view of our
own country-side that we had known all our lives.
After that the painter painted many pictures, and
we heard his name many times, though it was long
before we saw him again. But at last one day he
walked into our cottage, looking proud and happy, as
those who have done well must surely feel. He
told us how the picture he had painted, which he
had so nearly put away unfinished, had been sold
and hung up in a public gallery, where all could see
it. But the portrait of the child he had brought for
the child's mother, for he said none could value it as
she would. And then he told us how he owed most
of his fame to the old sampler that hung up over our
fireplace. For he had given up his picture in despair,
fearing he would gain nothing by it, but when he
read the words written on the sampler, he sat and
thought how gain and fame were small things to
seek, and that the knowledge that one had done
some good work would surely be sweeter far than
either. So he had taken out his picture and worked
at it again, trying hard with that, as with all after
work, to make it better and better, never wholly
satisfied with what he had done, and for ever with
each new thing he did, aiming higher and higher;

striving after that perfection which many seek yet none can hope to gain. And now," said the woman, looking up at the boy again, "all people know his name, and the knowledge he sought is his, and all other things are in his reach. He offered to buy the old sampler of us, and said he would keep it all his life; but my mother would not sell it, for she said it had been given to her from simple love, which no money can buy. Surely the painter is a great man!" and the woman stopped.

"Yes," said the boy, "he is a great man; but I think the cobbler was a great man too. Do you know what he was called?"

"I never heard his name," the woman answered, "but I suppose it was that by which his daughter went."

"Where did he live?" asked the boy.

"I do not know," the woman answered, "but what he was and where he lived do not concern us; it is what he did that has been of help and service to others; and what we are matters little, but what we do matters to all the world." Surely she was right, seeing how immortal is human action, be it good or ill? None of us can say that the good shall live and the bad shall die, and none of us can tell when we may be making history.

III.

"SURELY the things we can do matter little!" the boy said. "I cannot think that anything I can ever do will be of consequence."

"You cannot tell," said the woman, "and thus it is that we must be so careful."

"And why is what one does so much greater than what one is?" he asked absently, half forgetting the story she had just told him.

"Man must die," the woman answered sadly; "even the best loved and the greatest, and those who knew him and remember his face die also in their turn. So he who desires to live must fashion his own immortality out of what his hands shall find to do. And he whose ambition is highest has no wish to be remembered, save by those who loved him; but that his work shall be remembered, that is the desire of his soul."

"Many a man lives and works and dies," said the woman from the country, "without thought of anything save of doing his best in his day, glad and ready to help those about him, content to die when his turn comes, and never a thought of lying in wait for immortality."

"It steals on many a one unawares and wraps him round so softly he never knows that it is his!" said the young woman, taking up her sewing once more.

"I am not thinking of those," said the stranger, "but of those whom it never touches, and who have neither thought nor knowledge of it, and yet are as useful as any. One does not think of the stones hidden at the base, and yet the great tower rests on them, and but for them would never stand so high."

"Ah! but then it is surely a great thing to help a tower to stand," the spinner said. But the stranger did not seem to hear her, and went on—

"It is the simple-hearted folk, pure-lived and pure-thinking, who do well for love of doing well, and for love of those about them that help, each one in his place, to make the world so beautiful and life so sweet. Each one helps to make a whole, just as the little grains of sand make up the long sea-shore."

"But we were talking of great men," the boy said impatiently. "Did you ever know any?" he asked the stranger.

She was silent for a moment, and then she spoke, looking away from the boy, far off into the distance, as if the place she had come from lay beyond, and her thoughts were going home to it with every word she said.

"No," she said, "I have never known any that were called great; but once, years and years ago, I knew a scholar: he had more knowledge than any man for miles and miles round."

"Tell me about him," the boy said eagerly.

"He had studied all his life long," the stranger went on; "he knew all manner of languages, and had read all the books that were written in them. He was always studying : he shut himself up and saw no one, and talked to no one if he could help it, and learned more and more and more, and bought all strange and learned books to read, and at last I heard that there were few greater scholars than he. Many people went to his house; but even if he saw them, he did not say much, for he was always thinking of this strange science, and that new art, and of the books he was reading, and the language he was learning, so that he seemed to have no words for common use, and those who went to see him came away strangely impressed by his learning, and yet no wiser than they went."

"What did he do with his learning?" asked the boy. "Did he teach any?"

"No, he taught none: the simple people were afraid of him, for he knew so much and said so little. Even to learned men like himself he did not say much more; so they too went away disappointed."

"What did he do with his learning?"

"He did nothing with it, he never wrote it down, he never taught others; he just went on for ever taking in and never giving out; he was like a human cupboard——"

"He was just like a cupboard," laughed the boy. But the stranger frowned when she heard his laugh; it seemed as if the recollection of the scholar was painful to her.

"And one day," she went on, "a lock was put upon his lips, and he could never learn again, and could speak no more, for the key to the lock has never been found in this world; and so there was nothing more to be done with the scholar, and he was hidden away out of sight and sound for ever, and all his learning was locked up with him."

"Is that all?" asked the boy; but the stranger went on quickly, not seeming to hear him. "There was a blacksmith living in the same place with the scholar," she said. "He had a wife and children; he worked hard, as best he could, and was always

cheerful and hopeful, and had a helping hand and a
ready smile for all who looked for them, and for
many who had no thought of finding them. He died
at the same time as the scholar, and those who were
nearest to him would have died for love of him,
but that they knew it would be greater love still to
live for him. All the place was sadder and poorer
for his loss, and the best wish folk could wish his
sons was that they might grow up to be like him."

"But he was not a great man ; there are surely
many like him ? " the boy said.

"And he was lucky in his friends to be loved so
well," the spinner said.

"No, he was not a great man, and there are many
like him," the stranger said with a sigh. "But he
was worth considering ; it is the like of him that
have made the world worth living in for us, and will
make it worth living in for those that are to come. .
As for love," she said, looking at the spinner, "there
is always love somewhere for the heart that knows
how to bid it welcome ;" and she rose to go on her
way.

"But we were talking of greatness," the boy persisted.

"Yes, we were talking of greatness," she repeated

sadly. "Don't hanker after it or go seeking it; do what you can as best you can, and some day perhaps, without your knowing it, it will be looking over your shoulder;" and before any of them spoke again the stranger was journeying on into the distance.

LULLABY.

THE drowsy night is coming,
  The mist is on the heath;
Above the stars are shining,
  The glow-worms underneath.
The flowers for sleep are sighing,
  The bird is in its nest,
The daylight is all hidden
  With sunshine in the west.

The ladybird at sunset
  Went swiftly to her home;
The bats their wings are spreading,
  And quite prepared to roam.
And, hark ! the cricket singing
  His love-song to the skies,
Where all the stars are waiting
  To see you close your eyes.

L

They wish you all sweet slumber,
    They wish you all good night;
They'll tell the sun to rouse you
    When once again 'tis light.
And while you sleep, the roses
    May think your cheeks so fair
That, in the early morning,
    You'll find them resting there.

THE END.

Printed by R. & R. CLARK, *Edinburgh.*

MESSRS. MACMILLAN AND CO.'S

NEW BOOKS FOR CHILDREN.

MR. WALTER CRANE'S NEW BOOK

With upwards of 170 *New Pictures.*

Grimm's Fairy Tales. A Selection from the Household Stories, done into Pictures by WALTER CRANE. Crown 8vo. 6s.

* Also an Edition, limited to 250 Copies, printed on large paper. Royal 8vo. 21s.

"All should hail with gratitude this new picture-book, which we recommend to every nursery and schoolroom ; and not only to every nursery and schoolroom, but to every one who cares for good art."—*Spectator.*

New Coloured Picture-Book for Children.

The Horkey: a Provincial Ballad. By ROBERT BLOOMFIELD. Told in Coloured Pictures by GEORGE CRUIKSHANK. With an Address to Young Folks by F. C. BURNAND. 4to. 5s.

"The designs are marked by abundance of character and spirit in a style like that of Miss Kate Greenaway's best productions, and the colouring is nice and agreeable. They excel in character. . . . The book is one of the best we have yet received this season."—*The Athenæum.*

PEOPLE'S EDITIONS, profusely Illustrated, 6d. each.

Or, Complete in One Volume, Cloth, Medium 4to. 3s.

Tom Brown's Schooldays.

"A book that will amuse, delight, and elevate boys."—*Spectator.*

Waterton's Wanderings in South America.

"One of the most delightful books ever written."—*Saturday Review.*

Washington Irving's Old Christmas.

"One of the prettiest volumes we have seen."—*Saturday Review.*

Washington Irving's Bracebridge Hall.

"We cannot conceive a better present for young or old."—*The Globe.*

MACMILLAN'S BOOKS FOR THE YOUNG.

In Globe 8vo, Cloth elegant. Illustrated. 2s. 6d. *each.*

Pansie's Flour Bin. By the Author of " When I was a Little Girl." With Illustrations by ADRIAN STOKES.

Milly and Olly; or, A Holiday among the Mountains. By Mrs. T. H. WARD. With Illustrations by Mrs. ALMA TADEMA.

The Heroes of Asgard ; Tales from Scandinavian Mythology. By A. and E. KEARY.

When I was a Little Girl. By the Author of "St. Olave's," "Nine Years Old," etc.

A Storehouse of Stories. Edited by CHARLOTTE M. YONGE. 2 Vols.

The Story of a Fellow Soldier. By FRANCES AWDRY. (A Life of Bishop Patteson for the Young.) With Preface by CHARLOTTE M. YONGE.

Ruth and Her Friends.

Wandering Willie. By the Author of " Conrad the Squirrel." With a Frontispiece by Sir NOEL PATON.

Conrad the Squirrel. By the Author of " Effie's Friends," etc.

The White Rat, and Other Stories. By Lady BARKER. With Illustrations by W. J. HENNESSY.

Our Year. A Child's Book in Prose and Verse. By the Author of " John Halifax, Gentleman."

Little Sunshine's Holiday. By the Author of " John Halifax, Gentleman."

Agnes Hopetoun's Schools and Holidays. By Mrs. OLIPHANT.

The Runaway. By the Author of " Mrs. Jerningham's Journal."

Nine Years Old. By the Author of " When I was a Little Girl."

MACMILLAN AND CO., LONDON.

MESSRS. MACMILLAN AND CO.'S
PUBLICATIONS.

BOOKS FOR CHILDREN.

The Heroes: Greek Fairy Tales for my Children. By CHARLES KINGSLEY. New Edition. With Illustrations. Crown 8vo. 6s.

The Water Babies: A Fairy Tale for a Land Baby. By CHARLES KINGSLEY. With Illustrations by Sir NOEL PATON and P. SKELTON. New Edition. Crown 8vo. 6s.

Cast up by the Sea; or, The Adventures of Ned Gray. By Sir SAMUEL BAKER. Illustrated by HUARD. Eighth Edition. 8vo. 6s.

Alice's Adventures in Wonderland. By LEWIS CARROLL. With Illustrations by TENNIEL. Crown 8vo. 6s.

Through the Looking-Glass, and what Alice found there. By LEWIS CARROLL. With Illustrations by TENNIEL. Crown 8vo. 6s.

The Five Days' Entertainments at Wentworth Grange. A Book for Children. By F. T. PALGRAVE. With Illustrations by ARTHUR HUGHES. Small 4to, cloth extra. 6s.

Fairy Tales: Their Origin and Meaning, with some Account of the Dwellers in Fairyland. By J. THACKRAY BUNCE. Extra fcap. 8vo. 3s. 6d.

Stories from the History of Rome. By Mrs. BEESLY. Extra fcap. 8vo. 2s. 6d.

Cameos from English History. By the Author of "The Heir of Redclyffe." 4 vols. Extra fcap. 8vo. 5s. each. Vol. I. Rollo to Edward II.—II. The Wars in France.—III. The Wars of the Roses.—IV. Reformation Times.

Scouring of the White Horse; or, The Long Vacation Ramble of a London Clerk. By the Author of "Tom Brown's Schooldays." Illustrated by DOYLE. 10th Thousand. Imp. 16mo. 5s.

Storm Warriors; or, Lifeboat Work on the Goodwin Sands. By Rev. J. GILMORE. Crown 8vo. 6s.

History of the Lifeboat and its Work. By RICHARD LEWIS, of the Inner Temple, Barrister-at-Law. With numerous Illustrations. Second Edition. Crown 8vo. 5s.

MACMILLAN AND CO., LONDON.

MESSRS. MACMILLAN AND CO.'S
PUBLICATIONS.

BOOKS FOR PRESENTS.

NATURAL HISTORY AND TRAVELS.

Gilbert White's Natural History and Antiquities of
Selborne. New Edition. Edited, with Notes and Memoir, by FRANK BUCK-
LAND. Illustrated by Professor DELAMOTTE. Crown 8vo. 6s.

Waterton's Wanderings in South America and the
North-West of the United States, by CHARLES WATERTON. Edited by the
Rev. J. G. WOOD. With 100 Illustrations. Cheaper Edition. Crown 8vo. 6s.

By Sir SAMUEL BAKER, M.A., F.R.G.S.

Ismailia. A Narrative of the Expedition to Central Africa
for the Suppression of the Slave Trade, organised by Ismail, Khedive of Egypt.
With Illustrations by ZWECKER and DURAND. New and Cheaper Edition.
Crown 8vo. 6s.

The Nile Tributaries of Abyssinia and the Sword
Hunters of the Hamran Arabs. With Maps and Illustrations. Sixth and
Cheaper Edition. Crown 8vo. 6s.

The Albert N'Yanza Great Basin of the Nile, and
Explorations of the Nile Sources. With Maps and Illustrations. Fifth and
Cheaper Edition. Crown 8vo. 6s.

Log-Letters from the "Challenger." By Lord GEORGE
CAMPBELL. Fifth and Cheaper Edition, revised. Crown 8vo. 6s.

Greater Britain. A Record of Travel in English-speaking
Countries during 1866-67. (America, Australia, India.) By Sir CHARLES W.
DILKE, M.P. Sixth and Cheaper Edition. Crown 8vo. 6s.

A Narrative of a Year's Journey through Central
and Eastern Arabia, 1862-63. By W. G. PALGRAVE. With Map, Plans, and
Portrait of Author, engraved on Steel by JEENS. Crown 8vo. 6s.

A Ramble Round the World, 1871. By M. le Baron
de HÜBNER, formerly Ambassador and Minister. Translated by Lady HERBERT.
New and Cheaper Edition. With numerous Illustrations. Crown 8vo. 6s.

My Circular Notes. Extracts from Journals ; Letters sent
Home ; Geological and other Notes, written while Travelling Westwards round
the World, 1875. By J. R. CAMPBELL, Author of "Frost and Fire." Crown
8vo. 6s.

Tales of Old Travel Re-Narrated by HENRY KINGSLEY.
With Eight full-page Illustrations by HUARD. Fifth Edition. Crown 8vo. 5s.

Tales of Old Japan. By A. B. MITFORD. With Illustrations drawn and cut on Wood by Japanese Artists. New Edition. Crown 8vo.
6s.

MACMILLAN AND CO., LONDON.

Now Publishing in Crown 8vo. 4s. 6d. each Volume.

Macmillan's 4s. 6d. Series.

A New American Novel.

Mr. Isaacs: A Tale of Modern India. By F. MARION CRAWFORD.

Democracy: An American Novel.

*** Popular Edition, in paper wrapper. Crown 8vo. 1s.

Unknown to History: A Novel. By CHARLOTTE M. YONGE, Author of "The Heir of Redclyffe." 2 vols.

The Burgomaster's Wife: A Tale of the Siege of Leyden. By Dr. GEORG EBERS, Author of "The Egyptian Princess," etc. Translated by CLARA BELL.

Only a Word. By Dr. GEORG EBERS. Translated by CLARA BELL. *[Immediately.*

A Memoir of Daniel Macmillan. By THOMAS HUGHES, Q.C. With a Portrait engraved by C. H. JEENS. (Third Thousand.)

The Burman: His Life and Notions. By SHWAY YOE. 2 vols.

Lectures on Art. Delivered in support of the Society for Protection of Ancient Buildings. By REGD. STUART POOLE, Professor W. B. RICHMOND, E. J. POYNTER, R.A., J. T. MICKLE-THWAITE, and WILLIAM MORRIS.

MACMILLAN AND CO., LONDON.

MACMILLAN & CO.'S CATALOGUE of Works in BELLES LETTRES, including Poetry, Fiction, etc.

ADDISON, SELECTIONS FROM. By JOHN RICHARD GREEN, M.A., LL.D. (Golden Treasury Series.) 18mo. 4*s.* 6*d.*

ADVENTURES OF A BROWNIE, THE. By the Author of "John Halifax, Gentleman." With Illustrations by Mrs. ALLINGHAM. New Edition. Globe 8vo. 4*s.* 6*d.*

ALLINGHAM.—THE BALLAD BOOK. Edited by WILLIAM ALLINGHAM (Golden Treasury Series.) 18mo. 4*s.* 6*d.*

ALEXANDER, (C. F.)—THE SUNDAY BOOK OF POETRY FOR THE YOUNG. (Golden Treasury Series.) 18mo. 4*s.* 6*d.*

A .LITTLE PILGRIM : IN THE UNSEEN. Crown 8vo. 2*s.* 6*d.*

AN ANCIENT CITY, AND OTHER POEMS.—BY A NATIVE OF SURREY. Extra fcap. 8vo. 6*s.*

ANDERSON.-—BALLADS AND SONNETS. By ALEXANDER ANDERSON (Surfaceman). Extra fcap. 8vo. 5*s.*

ARCHER.—CHRISTINA NORTH. By E. M ARCHER. New and Cheaper Edition. Crown 8vo. 6*s.*
UNDER THE LIMES. Second and Cheaper Edition. Crown 8vo. 6*s.*

ARNOLD.—THE POETICAL WORKS OF MATTHEW ARNOLD. Vol. I. EARLY POEMS, NARRATIVE POEMS, AND SONNETS. Vol. II. LYRIC, DRAMATIC, AND ELEGIAC POEMS. New and Complete Edition. Two Vols. Crown 8vo. Price 7*s.* 6*d.* each.
SELECTED POEMS OF MATTHEW ARNOLD. With Vignette engraved by C. H. JEENS. (Golden Treasury Series.) 18mo. 4*s.* 6*d.* Large Paper Edition. Crown 8vo. 12*s.* 6*d.*

ART AT HOME SERIES.—Edited by W. J. LOFTIE, B.A.
A PLEA FOR ART IN THE HOUSE. With especial reference to the Economy of Collecting Works of Art, and the importance of Taste in Education and Morals. By W. J. LOFTIE, B.A. With Illustrations. Fifth Thousand. Crown 8vo. 2*s.* 6*d.*
SUGGESTIONS FOR HOUSE DECORATION IN PAINTING, WOOD-WORK, AND FURNITURE. By RHODA and AGNES GARRETT. With Illustrations. Sixth Thousand. Crown 8vo. 2*s.* 6*d.*

a

15,000. 10. 82.

ART AT HOME SERIES—*continued.*

MUSIC IN THE HOUSE. By JOHN HULLAH. With Illustrations. Fourth Thousand. Crown 8vo. 2s. 6d.

THE DRAWING-ROOM; ITS DECORATIONS AND FURNITURE. By Mrs. ORRINSMITH. Illustrated. Fifth Thousand. Crown 8vo. 2s. 6d.

THE DINING-ROOM. By MRS. LOFTIE. Illustrated. Fourth Thousand. Crown 8vo. 2s. 6d.

THE BED-ROOM AND BOUDOIR. By LADY BARKER. Illustrated. Fourth Thousand. Crown 8vo. 2s. 6d.

DRESS. By Mrs. OLIPHANT. Illustrated. Crown 8vo. 2s. 6d.

AMATEUR THEATRICALS. By WALTER H. POLLOCK and LADY POLLOCK. Illustrated by KATE GREENAWAY. Crown 8vo. 2s. 6d.

NEEDLEWORK. By ELIZABETH GLAISTER, Author of "Art Embroidery." Illustrated. Crown 8vo. 2s. 6d.

THE MINOR ARTS—PORCELAIN PAINTING, WOOD CARVING, STENCILLING, MODELLING, MOSAIC WORK, &c. By CHARLES G. LELAND. Illustrated. Crown 8vo. 2s. 6d.

THE LIBRARY. By ANDREW LANG. With a Chapter on *English Illustrated Books*, by AUSTIN DOBSON. Illustrated. Crown 8vo. 3s. 6d.

[Other Vols. in preparation.]

ATKINSON.—AN ART TOUR TO THE NORTHERN CAPITALS OF EUROPE By J. BEAVINGTON ATKINSON. 8vo. 12s.

ATTWELL (HENRY). A BOOK OF GOLDEN THOUGHTS. (Golden Treasury Series.) 18mo. 4s. 6d.

AUSTIN.—Works by ALFRED AUSTIN.

SAVONAROLA. A Tragedy. Crown 8vo. 7s. 6d.

SOLILOQUIES IN SONG. Crown 8vo. 6s.

AWDRY.—THE STORY OF A FELLOW SOLDIER. By FRANCES AWDRY. (A Life of Bishop Patteson for the Young.) With a Preface by CHARLOTTE M. YONGE. Globe 8vo. 2s. 6d.

BACON'S ESSAYS. Edited by W. ALDIS WRIGHT. (Golden Treasury Series.) 18mo. 4s. 6d.

BAKER.—CAST UP BY THE SEA; or, THE ADVENTURES OF NED GREY. By Sir SAMUEL BAKER, Pasha, F.R.G.S. With Illustrations by HUARD. Sixth Edition. Crown 8vo. cloth gilt. 6s.

BALLAD BOOK. — CHOICEST ANECDOTES AND SAYINGS. Edited by WILLIAM ALLINGHAM. (Golden Treasury Series.) 18mo. 4s. 6d.

BARKER (LADY).—Works by Lady BARKER:

A YEAR'S HOUSEKEEPING IN SOUTH AFRICA. With Illustrations. Cheaper Edition. Crown 8vo. 6s.

THE WHITE RAT and other Stories. Illustrated by W. J. HENNESSY. Globe 8vo. 2s. 6d.

BEESLY.—STORIES FROM THE HISTORY OF ROME. By Mrs. BEESLY. Fcap. 8vo. 2s. 6d.

BIÉKLAS.—LOUKIS LARAS; or, THE REMINISCENCES OF A CHIOTE MERCHANT DURING THE GREEK WAR OF INDE-PENDENCE. From the Greek of D. BIKÉLAS. Translated, with Introduction on the Rise and Development of Modern Greek Literature, by J. GENNADIUS, late Chargé d'Affaires at the Greek Legation in London. Crown 8vo. 7s. 6d.

BLACK (W.).—Works by W. BLACK, Author of "A Daughter of Heth" :
THE STRANGE ADVENTURES OF A PHAETON. Illustrated. Crown 8vo. 6s.
A PRINCESS OF THULE. Crown 8vo. 6s.
THE MAID OF KILLEENA, and other Stories. Crown 8vo. 6s.
MADCAP VIOLET. Crown 8vo. 6s.
GREEN PASTURES AND PICCADILLY. Cheaper Edition. Crown 8vo 6s.
MACLEOD OF DARE. With Illustrations. Cheaper Edition. Crown 8vo. 6s.
WHITE WINGS. A YACHTING ROMANCE. Cheaper Edition. Crown 8vo. 6s.
THE BEAUTIFUL WRETCH : THE FOUR MAC NICOLS: THE PUPIL OF AURELIUS. Cheaper Edition. Crown 8vo. 6s.
SHANDON BELLS. A Novel. Three Vols. Crown 8vo. [In Preparation.

BJÖRNSON.—SYNNÖVE SOLBAKKEN. Translated from the Norwegian of BJÖRNSTJERNE BJÖRNSON, by JULIE SUTTER. Crown 8vo. 6s.

BLACKIE.—Works by JOHN STUART BLACKIE, sometime Professor of Greek in the University of Edinburgh :—
THE WISE MEN OF GREECE. In a Series of Dramatic Dialogues. Crown 8vo. 9s.
LAY SERMONS. Crown 8vo. 6s.
GOETHE'S FAUST. Translated into English Verse, with Notes and Preliminary Remarks. By J. STUART BLACKIE, F.R.S.E. Crown 8vo. 9s.

BLAKISTON.—MODERN SOCIETY IN ITS RELIGIOUS AND SOCIAL ASPECTS. By PEYTON BLAKISTON, M.D., F.R.S. Crown 8vo. 5s.

BLOOMFIELD.—THE HORKEY: A Provincial Ballad. By ROBERT BLOOMFIELD. Told in Coloured Pictures by GEORGE CRUIKSHANK. With an Address to Young Folks by F. C. BURNAND. The Illustrations reproduced in Colours by Messrs. Clay, Sons, and Taylor. 4to. 5s.

BRAMSTON.—RALPH AND BRUNO. A Novel. By M. BRAMSTON. Two Vols. Crown 8vo. 21s.

BRIGHT.—Works by HENRY A. BRIGHT.
A YEAR IN A LANCASHIRE GARDEN. Second Edition. Crown 8vo. 3s. 6d.
THE ENGLISH FLOWER GARDEN. Crown 8vo 3s. 6d.

BRIMLEY.—ESSAYS. By the late Geɔrge Brimley, M.A., Librarian of Trinity College, Cambridge. Edited by W. G. Clark, M.A., late Fellow and Tutor of Trinity Collegᵉ, Cambridge. A new Edition. Globe 8vo. 5s.

Contents: Tennyson's Poems; Wordsworth's Poems; Poetry and Criticism; Carlyle's Life of Sterling; "Esmond": "Westward Ho!"; Wilson's "Noctes Ambrosianæ"; Comte's "Positive Philosophy," &c.

BROOKE.—THE FOOL OF QUALITY, or, THE HISTORY OF HENRY, EARL OF MORELAND. By Henry Brooke. Newly revised, with a Biographical Preface by the Rev. Charles Kingsley, M.A., Rector of Eversley. Crown 8vo. 6s.

BROOKE (S. A.).—RIQUET OF THE TUFT: A LOVE DRAMA. By the Rev. Stopford A. Brooke, M.A. Extra crown 8vo. 6s.

BROWNE (ᶜIR THOMAS).—RELIGIO MEDICI; Letter to a Friend, &c., and Christian Morals. Edited by W. A. Greenhill, M.D. 18mo. 4s. 6d. (Golden Treasury Series.)

BUNCE.—FAIRY TALES, THEIR ORIGIN AND MEANING. With some Account of the Dwellers in Fairy Land. By J. Thackray Bunce. Extra fcap. 8vo. 3s. 6d.

BUNYAN'S PILGRIM'S PROGRESS. (Golden Treasury Series.) 18mo. 4s. 6d.

BURKE.—LETTERS, TRACTS, AND SPEECHES ON IRISH AFFAIRS. By Edmund Burke. Arranged and Edited by Matthew Arnold, with a Preface. Crown 8vo. 6s.

BURNAND.—MY TIME, AND WHAT I'VE DONE WITH IT. By F. C. Burnand. Crown 8vo. 6s.

BURNETT.—Works by Frances Hodgson Burnett, Author of "That Lass o' Lowrie's":—

HAWORTH'S. A Novel. Crown 8vo. 6s.

LOUISIANA; and THAT LASS O' LOWRIE'S. Two Stories. Illustrated. Crown 8vo. 6s.

BURNS.—THE POETICAL WORKS OF ROBERT BURNS. Edited from the best printed and manuscript Authorities, with Glossarial Index and a Biographical Memoir, by Alexander Smith. Two Vols. Fcap. 8vo, hand-made paper with Portrait of Burns, and Vignette of the Twa Dogs, engraved by Shaw, and printed on India Paper. 12s.

COMPLETE WORKS OF. Edited with Memoir by Alexander Smith. (Globe Edition.) Globe 8vo. 3s. 6d.

BUTLER'S HUDIBRAS. Part I. Edited, with Introduction and Notes, by Alfred Milnes, M.A. Fcap. 8vo. 3s. 6d.

BYRON.—POETRY OF BYRON. Chosen and arranged by Matthew Arnold. (Golden Treasury Series.) 18mo. 4s. 6d. Large Paper Edition. Crown 8vo. 9s.

CARROLL.—Works by LEWIS CARROLL:—
ALICE'S ADVENTURES IN WONDERLAND. With Forty-two Illustrations by TENNIEL. 68th Thousand. Crown 8vo, cloth. 6s.
A GERMAN TRANSLATION OF THE SAME. With TENNIEL's Illustrations. Crown 8vo, gilt. 6s.
A FRENCH TRANSLATION OF THE SAME. With TENNIEL's Illustrations. Crown 8vo, gilt. 6s.
AN ITALIAN TRANSLATION OF THE SAME. By T. P. ROSSETTE. With TENNIEL's Illustrations. Crown 8vo. 6s.
THROUGH THE LOOKING-GLASS, AND WHAT ALICE FOUND THERE. With Fifty Illustrations by TENNIEL. Crown 8vo, gilt. 6s. 52nd Thousand.
THE HUNTING OF THE SNARK. An Agony in Eight Fits. With Nine Illustrations by H. HOLIDAY. Crown 8vo, cloth extra, gilt edges. 4s. 6d. 18th Thousand.
DOUBLETS. A Word Puzzle. 18mo. 2s.
PHANTASMAGORIA. A new Edition, with Illustrations, by W. B. FROST. Crown 8vo. [In the press.

CAUTLEY.—A CENTURY OF EMBLEMS. By G. S. CAUTLEY, Vicar of Nettleden, Author of "The After Glow," etc. With numerous Illustrations by LADY MARION ALFORD, REAR-ADMIRAL LORD W. COMPTON, the Ven. LORD A. COMPTON, R. BARNES, J. D. COOPER, and the Author. Pott 4to, cloth elegant, gilt elegant. 10s. 6d.

CAVALIER AND HIS LADY. Selections from the Works of the First Duke and Duchess of Newcastle. With an Introductory Essay by E. JENKINS. (Golden Treasury Series.) 18mo. 4s. 6d.

CHILDREN'S POETRY. By the author of "John Halifax, Gentleman." Extra Fcap. 8vo. 4s. 6d.

CHRISTMAS CAROL (A). Printed in Colours from Original Designs by Mr. and Mrs. TREVOR CRISPIN, with Illuminated Borders from MSS. of the 14th and 15th Centuries. Imp. 4to, cloth elegant. Cheaper Edition. 21s.

CHURCH (A. J.).—HORÆ TENNYSONIANÆ, Sive Eclogæ e Tennysono Latine redditæ. Cura A. J. CHURCH, A.M. Extra fcap. 8vo. 6s.

CLIFFORD.—ANYHOW STORIES—MORAL AND OTHERWISE. By Mrs. W. K. CLIFFORD. With Illustrations by DOROTHY TENNANT. Crown 8vo. 3s. 6d.

CLOUGH (ARTHUR HUGH).—THE POEMS AND PROSE REMAINS OF ARTHUR HUGH CLOUGH. With a Selection from his Letters, and a Memoir. Edited by his Wife. With Portrait. Two Vols. Crown 8vo. 21s.
THE POEMS OF ARTHUR HUGH CLOUGH, sometime Fellow of Oriel College, Oxford. Eighth Edition. Fcap. 8vo. 6s.

CLUNES.—THE STORY OF PAULINE: An Autobiography By G. C. CLUNES. Crown 8vo. 6s.

COLERIDGE.—HUGH CRICHTON'S ROMANCE. A Novel. By CHRISTABEL R. COLERIDGE. Second Edition. Crown 8vo. 6s.

COLLECTS OF THE CHURCH OF ENGLAND. With a beautifully Coloured Floral Design to each Collect, and Illuminated Cover. Crown 8vo. 12s. Also kept in various styles of morocco.

COLLIER.—A PRIMER OF ART. By JOHN COLLIER. 18mo. 1s.

COLQUHOUN.—RHYMES AND CHIMES. By F. S. COLQUHOUN (née F. S. FULLER MAITLAND). Extra fcap. 8vo. 2s. 6d.

COOPER.—SEBASTIAN. A Novel. By KATHERINE COOPER. Crown 8vo. 6s.

COWPER.—POETICAL WORKS. Edited, with Biographical Introduction, by Rev. W. BENHAM, B.D. (Globe Edition.) Globe 8vo. 3s. 6d.

CRANE—GRIMM'S FAIRY TALES: A Selection from the Household Stories. Translated from the German by LUCY CRANE, and done into Pictures by WALTER CRANE. Crown 8vo. 6s.

. Also an Edition. limited to 250 Copies, printed on large paper. Royal 8vo. 21s.

CRANE LECTURES ON ART AND THE FORMATION OF TASTE. By LUCY CRANE. With Illustrations by THOMAS and WALTER CRANE. Crown 8vo. [*Just ready.*

CRAWFORD—MR. ISAACS. A Tale of Modern India. By F. MARION CRAWFORD. Crown 8vo. 4s. 6d. [*In the press.*

DANTE ; AN ESSAY. By the Very Rev. R. W. CHURCH, D.C.L., Dean of St. Paul's. With a Translation of the "De Monarchiâ." By F. J. CHURCH. Crown 8vo. 6s.

THE "DE MONARCHIA." Separately. 8vo. 4s. 6d.

THE PURGATORY. Edited, with Translation and Notes, by A. J. BUTLER. Crown 8vo. 12s. 6d.

DAY.—BENGAL PEASANT LIFE. By the Rev. LAL BEHARI DAY. New Edition. Crown 8vo. 6s.

DAYS OF OLD ; STORIES FROM OLD ENGLISH |HISTORY. By the Author of " Ruth and Her Friends." New Edition. 18mo. 2s. 6d.

DEMOCRACY—An American Novel. Crown 8vo. 4s. 6d. Also a POPULAR EDITION, in Paper Wrapper, crown 8vo, price ONE SHILLING.

DE MORGAN (MARY).—THE NECKLACE OF THE PRINCESS FIORIMONDE, and other Stories. With 25 Illustrations by WALTER CRANE. Extra fcap. 8vo. 6s.

. Also an Edition printed by Messrs. R. and R. Clark, on hand-made paper, the plates, initial letters, head and tail pieces being printed on Indian paper and mounted in the text. Fcap. 4to. THE EDITION IS LIMITED TO ONE HUNDRED COPIES.

DEUTSCHE LYRIK. By Dr. BUCHHEIM. (Golden Treasury Series.) 18mo. 4s. 6d.

DICKENS'S DICTIONARY OF PARIS, 1882. An Unconventional Handbook. With |Maps, Plans, &c. 18mo. Paper cover, 1s. Cloth, 1s. 6d.

DICKENS'S DICTIONARY OF LONDON, 1882. (Fourth Year.) An Unconventional Handbook. With Maps, Plans, &c. 18mo. Paper cover, 1s. Cloth, 1s. 6d.

DICKENS'S DICTIONARY OF THE THAMES, 1882. An Unconventional Handbook. With Maps, Plans, &c. Paper cover, 1s. Cloth. 1s. 6d.

DICKENS'S CONTINENTAL A.B.C. RAILWAY GUIDE. Published on the first of each Month. 18mo. 1s.

DILLWYN (E. A.).—THE REBECCA RIOTER. A Story of Killay Life. Two Vols. Crown 8vo. 21*s.*

DOTTY, AND OTHER POEMS. By J. L. Extra fcap. 8vo. 3*s.* 6*d.*

DRYDEN.—POETICAL WORKS OF. Edited, with a Memoir, by W. D. CHRISTIE, M.A. (Globe Edition.) Globe 8vo. 3*s.* 6*d.*

DUFF (GRANT).—MISCELLANIES, POLITICAL and LITERARY. By the Right Hon. M. E. GRANT DUFF, M.P. 8vo. 10*s.* 6*d.*

DUNSMUIR (AMY).—VIDA; Study of a Girl. New Edition. Crown 8vo. 6*s.*

EBERS.—THE BURGOMASTER'S WIFE; a Tale of the Siege of Leyden. By Dr. GEORG EBERS, Author of "The Egyptian Princess," &c. Translated by CLARA BELL. Crown 8vo. 4*s.* 6*d.*

ELSIE ; A LOWLAND SKETCH. By A. C. M. Crown 8vo. 6*s.*

ENGLISH MEN OF LETTERS. Edited by JOHN MORLEY. Crown 8vo. 2*s.* 6*d.* each.

JOHNSON. By LESLIE STEPHEN.
SCOTT. By R. H. HUTTON.
GIBBON. By J. C. MORISON.
SHELLEY. By J. A. SYMONDS.
HUME. By Professor HUXLEY.
GOLDSMITH. By WILLIAM BLACK.
DEFOE. By W. MINTO.
BURNS. By Principal SHAIRP.
SPENSER. By the Very Rev. R. W. CHURCH, Dean of St. Paul's.
THACKERAY. By ANTHONY TROLLOPE.
BURKE. By JOHN MORLEY.
MILTON. By MARK PATTISON.
HAWTHORNE. By HENRY JAMES, Junr.
SOUTHEY. By Professor DOWDEN.
CHAUCER. By A. W. WARD.
COWPER. By GOLDWIN SMITH.
BUNYAN. By J. A. FROUDE.
LOCKE. By Professor FOWLER.
BYRON. By Professor NICHOL.
WORDSWORTH. By F. W. H. MYERS.
DRYDEN. BY GEORGE SAINTSBURY.
LANDOR. By Professor SIDNEY COLVIN.
DE QUINCEY. By Professor MASSON.
CHARLES LAMB. By Rev. ALFRED AINGER.
BENTLEY. By Professor D. C. JEBB.
CHARLES DICKENS. By A. W. WARD.
GRAY. By E. W. GOSSE.
SWIFT. By LESLIE STEPHEN.
STERNE. By H. D. TRAILL.
MACAULAY. By J. COTTER MORISON.
SHERIDAN. By Mrs. OLIPHANT.   [*In the press.*
[Other Volumes to follow.]

ESTELLE RUSSELL. By the Author of "The Private Life of Galilee New Edition. Crown 8vo. 6s.

EVANS.—Works by SEBASTIAN EVANS.

BROTHER FABIAN'S MANUSCRIPT, AND OTHER POEMS. Fcap 8vo, cloth. 6s.

IN THE STUDIO: A DECADE OF POEMS. Extra fcap. 8vo. 5s.

FAIRY BOOK. By the Author of "John Halifax, Gentleman" (Golden Treasury Series.) 18mo. 4s. 6d.

FAWCETT.—TALES IN POLITICAL ECONOMY. By MILLICENT G. FAWCETT, Author of "Political Economy for Beginners." Globe 8vo. 3s.

FLEMING.—Works by GEORGE FLEMING.

A NILE NOVEL. Third and Cheaper Edition. Crown 8vo. 6s.

MIRAGE. A Novel. Cheaper Elition. Crown 8vo. 6s.

THE HEAD OF MEDUSA. A Novel. Three Volumes. Crown 8vo. 31s. 6d.

FO'C'S'LE YARNS. -Including "BETSY LEE" AND OTHER POEMS. Crown 8vo. 7s. 6d.

FRASER-TYTLER.—SONGS IN MINOR KEYS. By C. C. FRASER-TYTLER (Mrs. EDWARD LIDDELL). 18mo. 6s.

FREEMAN.—Works by E. A. FREEMAN, D.C.L., LL.D.

HISTORICAL AND ARCHITECTURAL SKETCHES; CHIEFLY ITALIAN. With Illustrations by the Author. Crown 8vo. 10s. 6d.

SUBJECT AND NEIGHBOUR LANDS OF VENICE. Being a Companion Volume to "Historical and Architectural Sketches." With Illustrations. Crown 8vo. 10s. 6d.

GARNETT. — IDYLLS AND EPIGRAMS. Chiefly from the Greek Anthology. By RICHARD GARNETT. Fcap. 8vo. 2s. 6d.

GILMORE.—STORM WARRIORS; or, LIFE-BOAT WORK ON THE GOODWIN SANDS. By the Rev. JOHN GILMORE, M.A., Vicar of St. Luke's, Lower Norwood, Surrey, Author of "The Ramsgate Life-Boat," in "Macmillan's Magazine." Second Edition. Crown 8vo. 6s.

GLOBE LIBRARY.—Globe 8vo. Cloth. 3s. 6d. each.

SHAKESPEARE'S COMPLETE WORKS. Edited by W. G. CLARK, M.A., and W. ALDIS WRIGHT, M.A., of Trinity College, Cambridge, Editors of the "Cambridge Shakespeare." With Glossary.

SPENSER'S COMPLETE WORKS. Edited from the Original Editions and Manuscripts, by R. MORRIS, with a Memoir by J. W. HALES. M.A. With Glossary.

SIR WALTER SCOTT'S POETICAL WORKS. Edited with a Biographical and Critical Memoir by FRANCIS TURNER PALGRAVE, and copious Notes.

GLOBE LIBRARY—*continued.*

COMPLETE WORKS OF ROBERT BURNS.—THE POEMS, SONGS, AND LETTERS, edited from the best Printed and Manuscript Authorities, with Glossarial Index, Notes, and a Biographical Memoir by ALEXANDER SMITH.

ROBINSON CRUSOE Edited after the Original Editions, with a Biographical Introduction by HENRY KINGSLEY.

GOLDSMITH'S MISCELLANEOUS WORKS. Edited, with Biographical Introduction by Professor MASSON.

POPE'S POETICAL WORKS. Edited, with Notes and Introductory Memoir, by ADOLPHUS WILLIAM WARD, M.A., Fellow of St. Peter's College, Cambridge, and Professor of History in Owens College, Manchester. .

DRYDEN'S POETICAL WORKS. Edited, with a Memoir, Revised Text and Notes, by W. D. CHRISTIE, M.A., of Trinity College, Cambridge.

COWPER'S POETICAL WORKS. Edited, with Notes and Biographical Introduction, by Rev. WILLIAM BENHAM, B.D.

MORTE D'ARTHUR.—SIR THOMAS MALORY'S BOOK OF KING ARTHUR AND OF HIS NOBLE KNIGHTS OF THE ROUND TABLE. The original Edition of CAXTON, revised for Modern Use. With an Introduction by Sir EDWARD STRACHEY, Bart.

THE WORKS OF VIRGIL. Rendered into English Prose, with Introductions, Notes, Running Analysis, and an Index. By JAMES LONDSDALE, M.A., late Fellow and Tutor of Balliol College, Oxford, and Classical Professor in King's College, London ; and SAMUEL LEE, M.A., Latin Lecturer at University College, London

THE WORKS OF HORACE. Rendered into English Prose with Introductions, Running Analysis, Notes and Index. By JOHN LONDSDALE, M.A., and SAMUEL LEE, M.A.

MILTON'S POETICAL WORKS, Edited, with Introductions, by Professor MASSON.

GOLDEN TREASURY SERIES.—Uniformly printed in 18mo., with Vignette Titles by J. E. MILLAIS, R.A., T. WOOLNER, W. HOLMAN HUNT, Sir NOEL PATON, ARTHUR HUGHES, &c. Engraved on Steel by JEENS, &c. Bound in extra cloth. 4s. 6d. each volume.

THE GOLDEN TREASURY OF THE BEST SONGS AND LYRICAL POEMS IN THE ENGLISH LANGUAGE. Selected and arranged, with Notes, by FRANCIS TURNER PALGRAVE.

THE CHILDREN'S GARLAND FROM THE BEST POETS. Selected and arranged by COVENTRY PATMORE.

THE BOOK OF PRAISE. From the best English Hymn Writers. Selected and arranged by LORD SELBORNE. *A New and Enlarged Edition.*

THE FAIRY BOOK ; the Best Popular Fairy Stories. Selected and rendered anew by the Author of " John Halifax, Gentleman."

THE BALLAD BOOK. A Selection of the Choicest British Ballads. Edited by WILLIAM ALLINGHAM.

THE JEST BOOK. The Choicest Anecdotes and Sayings. Selected and arranged by MARK LEMON.

GOLDEN TREASURY SERIES—*continued.*

BACON'S ESSAYS AND COLOURS OF GOOD AND EVIL. With Notes and Glossarial Index. By W. ALDIS WRIGHT, M.A.

THE PILGRIM'S PROGRESS from this World to that which is to come. By JOHN BUNYAN.

THE SUNDAY BOOK OF POETRY FOR THE YOUNG. Selected and arranged by C. F. ALEXANDER.

A BOOK OF GOLDEN DEEDS of All Times and All Countries gathered and narrated anew. By the Author of "The Heir of Redclyffe."

THE ADVENTURES OF ROBINSON CRUSOE. Edited from the Original Edition by J. W. CLARK, M.A., Fellow of Trinity College, Cambridge.

THE REPUBLIC OF PLATO. Translated into English, with Notes, by J. Ll DAVIES, M.A. and D. J. VAUGHAN, M.A.

THE SONG BOOK. Words and Tunes from the best Poets and Musicians. Selected and arranged by JOHN HULLAH, Professor of Vocal Music in King's College, London.

LA LYRE FRANÇAISE. Selected and arranged, with Notes, by GUSTAVE MASSON, French Master in Harrow School.

TOM BROWN'S SCHOOLDAYS. BY AN OLD BOY.

A BOOK OF WORTHIES. Gathered from the Old Histories and written anew by the Author of "The Heir of Redclyffe." With Vignette.

A BOOK OF GOLDEN THOUGHTS. By HENRY ATTWELL, Knight of the Order of the Oak Crown.

GUESSES AT TRUTH. By Two BROTHERS. New Edition.

THE CAVALIER AND HIS LADY. Selections from the Works of the First Duke and Duchess of Newcastle. With an Introductory Essay by EDWARD JENKINS, Author of "Ginx's Baby," &c.

SCOTTISH SONG. A Selection of the Choicest Lyrics of Scotland. Compiled and arranged, with brief Notes, by MARY CARLYLE AITKEN.

DEUTSCHE LYRIK. The Golden Treasury of the best German Lyrical Poems, selected and arranged with Notes and Literary Introduction. By Dr. BUCHHEIM.

ROBERT HERRICK.—SELECTIONS FROM THE LYRICAL POEMS OF. Arranged with Notes by F. T. PALGRAVE.

POEMS OF PLACES. Edited by H. W. LONGFELLOW. England and Wales. Two Vols.

MATTHEW ARNOLD'S SELECTED POEMS. Also a Large Paper Edition. Crown 8vo. 12s. 6d.

THE STORY OF THE CHRISTIANS AND MOORS IN SPAIN. By CHARLOTTE M. YONGE. With a Vignette by HOLMAN HUNT.

LAMB'S TALES FROM SHAKESPEARE. Edited, with Preface, by the Rev. ALFRED AINGER, Reader at the Temple.

WORDSWORTH'S SELECT POEMS. Chosen and Edited, with Preface, by MATTHEW ARNOLD. Also a Large Paper Edition. Crown 8vo. 9s.

SHAKESPEARE'S SONGS AND SONNETS. Edited, with Notes, by FRANCIS TURNER PALGRAVE.

GOLDEN TREASURY SERIES—*continued.*

SELECTIONS FROM ADDISON. Edited by JOHN RICHARD GREEN.

SELECTIONS FROM SHELLEY. Edited by STOPFORD A. BROOKE. Also Large Paper Edition. Crown 8vo. 12s. 6d.

POETRY OF BYRON. Chosen and arranged by MATTHEW ARNOLD. Also a Large Paper Edition. Crown 8vo. 9s.

SIR THOMAS BROWNE'S RELIGIO MEDICI ; Letter to a Friend, &c., and Christian Morals. Edited by W. A. GREENHILL, M.D., Oxon.

MOHAMMAD, THE SPEECHES AND TABLE-TALK OF THE PROPHET. Chosen and Translated by STANLEY LANE-POOLE.

WALTER SAVAGE LANDOR, Selections from the Writings of. Arranged and Edited by Professor SIDNEY COLVIN.

GOLDSMITH.—MISCELLANEOUS WORKS. Edited with Biographical Introduction, by Professor MASSON. (Globe Edition.) Globe 8vo. 3s. 6d.

GOETHE'S FAUST. Translated into English Verse, with Notes and Preliminary Remarks, by JOHN STUART BLACKIE, F.R.S.E., sometime Professor of Greek in the University of Edinburgh. Crown 8vo. 9s.

GRIMM'S FAIRY TALES. A Selection from the Household Stories. Translated from the German by LUCY CRANE, and done into Pictures by WALTER CRANE. Crown 8vo. 6s.
. Also an Edition, limited to 250 Copies, printed on large paper. Royal 8vo. 21s.

GUESSES AT TRUTH. By Two BROTHERS. (Golden Treasury Series.) 18mo. 4s. 6d.

HAMERTON.—Works by P. G. HAMERTON.

ETCHING AND ETCHERS. Illustrated with Forty-eight new Etchings. Third Edition, revised. Columbier 8vo.

A PAINTER'S CAMP IN THE HIGHLANDS. Second and Cheaper Edition One Vol. Extra fcap. 8vo. 6s.

THE INTELLECTUAL LIFE. With Portrait of LEONARDO DA VINCI, etched by LEOPOLD FLAMENG. Second Edition. Crown 8vo. 10s. 6d.

THOUGHTS ABOUT ART. New Edition, Revised, with Notes and Introduction. Crown 8vo. 8s. 6d.

HARRY. A POEM. By the Author of "Mrs. Jerningham's Journal." Extra fcap. 8vo. 3s. 6d.

HAWTHORNE (JULIAN).—Works by JULIAN HAWTHORNE.

THE LAUGHING MILL ; and Other Stories. Cheaper Edition. Crown 8vo. 6s.

FORTUNE'S FOOL. A Novel. By JULIAN HAWTHORNE, Author of "The Laughing Mill, and other Stories," &c. 3 vols. Crown 8vo. [*In the press.*

HEINE.—SELECTIONS FROM THE POETICAL WORKS OF HEINRICH HEINE. Translated into English. Crown 8vo. 4s. 6d.

A TRIP TO THE BROCKEN. By HEINRICH HEINE. Translated by R. McLINTOCK. Crown 8vo. 3s. 6d.

HERRICK (ROBERT).—SELECTIONS FROM THE LYRICAL POEMS OF. Arranged with Notes by F. T. PALGRAVE. (Golden Treasury Series.) 18mo. 4s. 6d.

HIGGINSON.—MALBONE; An Oldport Romance. By T. W. Higginson. Fcap. 8vo. 2s. 6d.

HILDA AMONG THE BROKEN GODS. By the Author of "Olrig Grange." Extra fcap. 8vo. 7s. 6d.

HOOPER AND PHILLIPS.—A MANUAL OF MARKS ON POTTERY AND PORCELAIN. A Dictionary of Easy Reference. By W. H. Hooper and W. C. Phillips. With numerous Illustrations. Second Edition, revised. 16mo. 4s. 6d.

HOLLWAY-CALTHROP.—PALADIN AND SARACEN: Stories from Ariosto. By H. C. Hollway-Calthrop. With Illustrations by Mrs. Arthur Lemon, engraved by O. Lacour. Crown 8vo. 6s.

HOPE.—NOTES AND THOUGHTS ON GARDENS AND WOODLANDS. Written chiefly for Amateurs. By the late Frances Jane Hope, Wardie Lodge, near Edinburgh. Edited by Anne J. Hope Johnstone. Crown 8vo. 6s.

HOPKINS.—ROSE TURQUAND. A Novel. By Ellice Hopkins. Cheaper Edition. Crown 8vo. 6s.

HORACE.—WORD FOR WORD FROM HORACE. The Odes literally versified. By W. T. Thornton, C.B. Crown 8vo. 7s. 6d.
WORKS OF. Rendered into English Prose by John Lonsdale, M.A. and Samuel Lee, M.A. (Globe Edition.) Globe 8vo. 3s. 6d

HUNT.—TALKS ABOUT ART. By William Hunt. With a Letter by J. E. Millais. Second Edition. Crown 8vo. 3s. 6d.

IRVING.—Works by Washington Irving.

OLD CHRISTMAS From the Sketch Book. With upwards of 100 Illustrations by Randolph Caldecott, engraved by J. D. Cooper Second Edition. Crown 8vo, cloth elegant. 6s. People's Sixpenny Edition. Illustrated. Medium 4to. 6d.

BRACEBRIDGE HALL. With 120 Illustrations by R. Caldecott. Crown 8vo, cloth gilt. 6s. People's Sixpenny Edition. Illustrated. Medium 4to. 6d.

JAMES.—Works by Henry James, jun.
THE PORTRAIT OF A LADY. Cheaper Edition Crown 8vo. 6s.
WASHINGTON SQUARE; THE PENSION BEAUREPAS; A BUNDLE OF LETTERS. Cheaper Edition Crown 8vo. 6s.
THE EUROPEANS. A Novel. Cheaper Edition. Crown 8vo. 6s.
THE AMERICAN. Crown 8vo. 6s.
DAISY MILLER: AN INTERNATIONAL EPISODE: FOUR MEETINGS. Crown 8vo. 6s.
RODERICK HUDSON. Crown 8vo. 6s.
THE MADONNA OF THE FUTURE; and other Tales. Crown 8vo. 6s.

JOUBERT.—PENSÉES OF JOUBERT. Selected and Translated with the Original French appended, by Henry Attwell, Knight of the Order of the Oak Crown. Crown 8vo. 5s.

KEARY (A.).—Works by ANNIE KEARY.

CASTLE DALY; THE STORY OF AN IRISH HOME THIRTY YEARS AGO. New Edition. Crown 8vo. 6s.

JANET'S HOME. New Edition. Crown 8vo. 6s.

CLEMENCY FRANKLYN. New Edition. Crown 8vo. 6s.

OLDBURY. New and Cheaper Edition. Crown 8vo. 6s.

A YORK AND A LANCASTER ROSE. Crown 8vo. 6s.

A DOUBTING HEART. New Edition. Crown 8vo. 6s.

THE HEROES OF ASGARD. Globe 8vo. 2s. 6d.

KEARY (E.).—THE MAGIC VALLEY; or, PATIENT ANTOINE. With Illustrations by E. V. B. Globe 8vo. gilt. 4s. 6d.

KINGSLEY'S (CHARLES) NOVELS.—EVERSLEY EDITION

WESTWARD HO! 2 Vols. Globe 8vo. 10s.

TWO YEARS AGO. 2 Vols. Globe 8vo. 10s.

HYPATIA. 2 Vols. Globe 8vo. 10s.

YEAST. 1 Vol. Globe 8vo. 5s.

ALTON LOCKE. 2 Vols. Globe 8vo. 10s.

HEREWARD THE WAKE. 2 Vols. Globe 8vo. 10s.

KINGSLEY.—Works by the Rev. CHARLES KINGSLEY, M.A., Rector of Eversley, and Canon of Westminster. Collected Edition. 6s. each.

POEMS; including the Saint's Tragedy, Andromeda, Songs, Ballads, &c. Complete Collected Edition.

YEAST; a Problem.

ALTON LOCKE. New Edition. With a Prefatory Memoir by THOMAS HUGHES, Q.C., and Portrait of the Author.

HYPATIA; or, NEW FOES WITH AN OLD FACE.

GLAUCUS; or, THE WONDERS OF THE SEA-SHORE. With Coloured Illustrations.

WESTWARD HO! or, THE VOYAGES AND ADVENTURES OF SIR AMYAS LEIGH.

THE HEROES; or, GREEK FAIRY TALES FOR MY CHILDREN. With Illustrations.

TWO YEARS AGO.

THE WATER BABIES. A Fairy Tale for a Land Baby. With Illustrations by Sir NOEL PATON, R.S.A., and P. SKELTON.

THE ROMAN AND THE TEUTON. A Series of Lectures delivered before the University of Cambridge. With Preface by Professor MAX MÜLLER.

HEREWARD THE WAKE—LAST OF THE ENGLISH.

THE HERMITS.

MADAM HOW AND LADY WHY; or, FIRST LESSONS IN EARTH-LORE FOR CHILDREN.

AT LAST; A CHRISTMAS IN THE WEST INDIES. Illustrated.

PROSE IDYLLS. NEW AND OLD.

PLAYS AND PURITANS; and other HISTORICAL ESSAYS. With Portrait of Sir WALTER RALEIGH.

KINGSLEY (C.).—*continued.*

HISTORICAL LECTURES AND ESSAYS.
SANITARY AND SOCIAL LECTURES AND ESSAYS.
SCIENTIFIC LECTURES AND ESSAYS.
LITERARY AND GENERAL LECTURES.
HEALTH AND EDUCATION. New Edition. Crown 8vo. 6s.
PHAETHON; or, LOOSE THOUGHTS FOR LOOSE THINKERS. Crown 8vo. 2s.
TOWN GEOLOGY. Crown 8vo. 5s.
SELECTIONS FROM SOME OF THE WRITINGS OF THE REV. CHARLES KINGSLEY. Crown 8vo. 6s.
OUT OF THE DEEP. Words for the Sorrowful, from the writings of CHARLES KINGSLEY. Extra fcap. 8vo. 3s. 6d.

KINGSLEY (H.).—TALES OF OLD TRAVEL. Re-narrated by HENRY KINGSLEY. With Eight full-page Illustrations by HUARD. Fifth Edition. Crown 8vo, cloth, extra gilt. 5s.

KNOX.—SONGS OF CONSOLATION. By ISA CRAIG KNOX. Extra fcap. 8vo, cloth extra, gilt edges. 4s. 6d.

LAMB'S (CHARLES) TALES FROM SHAKESPEARE. Edited, with Preface, by the Rev. A. AINGER. (Golden Treasury Series.) 18mo. 4s. 6d.

LANDOR (WALTER SAVAGE).—SELECTIONS FROM THE WRITINGS OF WALTER SAVAGE LANDOR. Arranged and Edited by Professor SIDNEY COLVIN. With Portrait. 18mo. 4s. 6d. (Golden Treasury Series.)

LEADING CASES DONE INTO ENGLISH. By an Apprentice of Lincoln's Inn. Third Edition. Crown 8vo. 2s. 6d.

LÉCTURES ON ART.—Delivered in Support of the Society for Protection of Ancient Buildings. By REGD. STUART POOLE, Professor W. B. RICHMOND, E. J. POYNTER, R.A., J. T. MICKLETHWAITE, and WILLIAM MORRIS. Crown 8vo. 4s. 6d.

LEMON (MARK).—THE JEST BOOK. (Golden Treasury Series. 18mo. 4s. 6d.

LIFE AND TIMES OF CONRAD THE SQUIRREL. A Story for Children. By the Author of "Wandering Willie," "Effie's Friends," &c. With a Frontispiece by R. FARREN. Second Edition. Crown 8vo. 3s. 6d.

LITTLE ESTELLA, and other FAIRY TALES FOR THE YOUNG. 18mo, cloth extra. 2s 6d.

LITTLE SUNSHINE'S HOLIDAY.—By the Author of "John Halifax, Gentleman." With Illustrations. Globe 8vo. 2s. 6d.

LOFTIE.—FORTY-SIX SOCIAL TWITTERS. By Mrs. LOFTIE. Second Edition. 16mo. 2s. 6d.

LORNE.—Works by the MARQUIS OF LORNE:—

GUIDO AND LITA: A TALE OF THE RIVIERA. A Poem. Third Edition. Small 4to, cloth elegant. With Illustrations. 7s. 6d.

THE BOOK OF THE PSALMS; LITERALLY RENDERED IN VERSE. With Three Illustrations. Third Edition. Crown 8vo. 7s. 6d.

LOWELL.—COMPLETE POETICAL WORKS of JAMES RUSSELL LOWELL. With Portrait, engraved by JEENS. 18mo, cloth extra. 4s. 6d.

LYTTELTON.—Works by LORD LYTTELTON.

THE "COMUS" OF MILTON, rendered into Greek Verse. Extra fcap. 8vo. 5s.

THE "SAMSON AGONISTES" OF MILTON, rendered into Greek Verse. Extra fcap. 8vo. 6s. 6d.

MACLAREN.—THE FAIRY FAMILY. A Series of Ballads and Metrical Tales illustrating the Fairy Mythology of Europe. By ARCHIBALD MACLAREN. With Frontispiece, Illustrated Title, and Vignette. Crown 8vo, gilt. 5s.

MACMILLAN'S BOOKS FOR THE YOUNG.—In Globe 8vo, cloth elegant. Illustrated, 2s. 6d. each :—

WANDERING WILLIE. By the Author of "Conrad the Squirrel." With a Frontispiece by Sir NOEL PATON. Globe 8vo.

THE WHITE RAT, AND OTHER STORIES. By LADY BARKER. With Illustrations by W. J. HENNESSY. Globe 8vo.

PANSIE'S FLOUR BIN. By the Author of "When I was a Little Girl." With Illustrations by ADRIAN STOKES. Globe 8vo.

MILLY AND OLLY; or, A Holiday among the Mountains. By Mrs. T. H. WARD. With Illustrations by Mrs. ALMA TADEMA. Globe 8vo.

THE HEROES OF ASGARD; Tales from Scandinavian Mythology. By A. and E. KEARY.

WHEN I WAS A LITTLE GIRL. By the Author of "St. Olave's," "Nine Years Old," &c.

A STOREHOUSE OF STORIES. Edited by CHARLOTTE M. YONGE, Author of "The Heir of Redclyffe." Two Vols.

THE STORY OF A FELLOW-SOLDIER. By FRANCES AWDRY. (A Life of Bishop Patteson for the Young.) With Preface by CHARLOTTE M. YONGE.

AGNES HOPETOUN'S SCHOOLS AND HOLIDAYS. By Mrs. OLIPHANT.

RUTH AND HER FRIENDS. A Story for Girls.

THE RUNAWAY. By the Author of "Mrs. Jerningham's Journal."

OUR YEAR. A Child's Book in Prose and Verse. By the Author of "John Halifax, Gentleman."

LITTLE SUNSHINE'S HOLIDAY. By the Author of "John Halifax, Gentleman."

NINE YEARS OLD. By the Author of "When I was a Little Girl."

MACMILLAN'S MAGAZINE.—Published Monthly. Price 1s. Vols I. to XLVI. are now ready. 7s. 6d. each.

MACMILLAN'S POPULAR NOVELS.—In Crown 8vo, cloth.
Price 6s. each Volume :—

By William Black.

A PRINCESS OF THULE.

MADCAP VIOLET.

THE MAID OF KILLEENA; and other Tales.

THE STRANGE ADVENTURES OF A PHAETON. Illustrated.

GREEN PASTURES AND PIC-CADILLY.

MACLEOD OF DARE. Illustrated.

WHITE WINGS. A Yachting Romance.

THE BEAUTIFUL WRETCH : THE FOUR MAC NICOLS: THE PUPIL OF AURELIUS.

By Charles Kingsley.

TWO YEARS AGO.

"WESTWARD HO!"

ALTON LOCKE. With Portrait.

HYPATIA.

YEAST.

HEREWARD THE WAKE.

By the Author of "John Halifax, Gentleman."

THE HEAD OF THE FAMILY. Illustrated.

THE OGILVIES. Illustrated.

AGATHA'S HUSBAND. Illustrated.

OLIVE. Illustrated.

MY MOTHER AND I. Illustrated.

By Charlotte M. Yonge.

THE HEIR OF REDCLYFFE. With Illustrations.

HEARTSEASE. With Illustrations.

THE DAISY CHAIN. With Illustrations.

THE TRIAL: More Links in the Daisy Chain. With Illustrations.

HOPES AND FEARS. Illustrated.

DYNEVOR TERRACE. With Illustrations.

MY YOUNG ALCIDES. Illustrated.

THE PILLARS OF THE HOUSE. Two Vols. Illustrated.

CLEVER WOMAN OF THE FAMILY. Illustrated.

THE YOUNG STEPMOTHER. Illustrated.

THE DOVE IN THE EAGLE'S NEST. Illustrated.

THE CAGED LION. Illustrated.

THE CHAPLET OF PEARLS. Illustrated.

LADY HESTER, and THE DANVERS PAPERS. Illustrated.

THE THREE BRIDES. Illustrated.

MAGNUM BONUM. Illustrated.

LOVE AND LIFE. Illustrated.

By Frances H. Burnett.

HAWORTH'S.

"LOUISIANA" and "THAT LASS O' LOWRIE'S." Two Stories. Illustrated,

By Lady Augusta Noel.

OWEN GWYNNE'S GREAT WORK.

FROM GENERATION TO GENERATION.

MACMILLAN'S POPULAR NOVELS—*continued.*

By Mrs. Oliphant.

YOUNG MUSGRAVE. | A SON OF THE SOIL.
THE CURATE IN CHARGE. | A BELEAGUERED CITY.
HE THAT WILL NOT WHEN HE MAY.

By Annie Keary.

CASTLE DALY. | CLEMENCY FRANKLYN.
OLDBURY. | A YORK AND A LANCASTER ROSE.
JANET'S HOME. | A DOUBTING HEART.

By George Fleming.

A NILE NOVEL. | MIRAGE.

By Henry James, Junr.

THE EUROPEANS. | THE MADONNA OF THE FUTURE, and other Tales.
THE AMERICAN. |
DAISY MILLER · AN INTERNA-TIONAL EPISODE: FOUR MEETINGS. | WASHINGTON SQUARE: THE PENSION BEAUREPAS: A BUNDLE OF LETTERS.
RODERICK HUDSON. | THE PORTRAIT OF A LADY.

By the Author of "Hogan, M.P."

HOGAN, M.P. | CHRISTY CAREW.
THE HONOURABLE MISS FER-RARD. | FLITTERS, TATTERS, AND THE COUNSELLOR: WEEDS: AND OTHER SKETCHES.

TOM BROWN'S SCHOOLDAYS.
TOM BROWN AT OXFORD.
THE FOOL OF QUALITY. By H. Brooke.
REALMAH. By the Author of "Friends in Council."
PATTY. By Mrs. Macquoid.
THE BERKSHIRE LADY. By Mrs. Macquoid.
HUGH CRICHTON'S ROMANCE. By C. R. Coleridge.
MY TIME, AND WHAT I'VE DONE WITH IT. By F. C. Burnand.
ROSE TURQUAND. By Ellice Hopkins.

OLD SIR DOUGLAS. By the Hon. Mrs. Norton.
SEBASTIAN. By Katharine Cooper.
THE LAUGHING MILL; and other Tales. By Julian Hawthorne.
THE HARBOUR BAR.
CHRISTINA NORTH. By E. M. Archer.
UNDER THE LIMES. By E. M. Archer.
BENGAL PEASANT LIFE. By Lal Behari Day.
VIRGIN SOIL. By Tourguénief.
VIDA. The Study of a Girl. By Amy Dunsmuir.

b

MACMILLAN'S TWO SHILLING NOVELS :—

By the Author of "John Halifax, Gentleman."

THE OGILVIES.   AGATHA'S HUSBAND.
THE HEAD OF THE FAMILY.
OLIVE.   TWO MARRIAGES.

MACQUOID.—Works by KATHARINE S. MACQUOID.

PATTY. Third and Cheaper Edition. Crown 8vo. 6s.

THE BERKSHIRE LADY. Crown 8vo. 6s.

MAGUIRE.—YOUNG PRINCE MARIGOLD, AND OTHER FAIRY STORIES. By the late JOHN FRANCIS MAGUIRE, M.P. Illustrated by S. E. WALLER. Globe 8vo, gilt. 4s. 6d.

MAHAFFY.—Works by J. P. MAHAFFY, M.A., Fellow of Trinity College, Dublin :—

SOCIAL LIFE IN GREECE FROM HOMER TO MENANDER. Fourth Edition, enlarged. with New Chapter on Greek Art. Crown 8vo. 9s.

RAMBLES AND STUDIES IN GREECE. Illustrated. Second Edition, revised and enlarged, with Map. Crown 8vo. 10s. 6d.

THE DECAY OF MODERN PREACHING. An Essay. Crown 8vo. 3s. 6d.

MALET.—MRS. LORIMER. A Novel. By LUCAS MALET. Two Vols. Globe 8vo.   [*Immediately.*

MOHAMMAD, SPEECHES AND TABLE-TALK OF THE PROPHET. Chosen and Translated by STANLEY LANE-POOLE. 18mo. 4s. 6d. (Golden Treasury Series.)

MASSON (GUSTAVE).—LA LYRE FRANÇAISE. Selected and arranged with Notes. (Golden Treasury Series.) 18mo. 4s. 6d.

MASSON (Mrs.).—THREE CENTURIES OF ENGLISH POETRY: being selections from Chaucer to Herrick, with Introductions and Notes by Mrs. MASSON and a general Introduction by Professor MASSON. Extra fcap. 8vo. 3s. 6d.

MASSON (Professor).—Works by DAVID MASSON, M.A., Professor of Rhetoric and English Literature in the University of Edinburgh.

WORDSWORTH, SHELLEY, KEATS, AND OTHER ESSAYS. Crown 8vo. 5s.

CHATTERTON: A Story of the Year 1770. Crown 8vo. 5s.

THE THREE DEVILS: LUTHER'S, MILTON'S AND GOETHE'S; and other Essays. Crown 8vo. 5s.

MAZINI.—IN THE GOLDEN SHELL: A Story of Palermo. By LINDA MAZINI. With Illustrations. Globe 8vo, cloth gilt. 4s. 6d.

MERIVALE.—KEATS' HYPERION, rendered into Latin Verse. By C. MERIVALE, B.D. Second Edition. Extra fcap. 8vo. 3s. 6d.

MILNER.—THE LILY OF LUMLEY. By EDITH MILNER. Crown 8vo. 7s. 6d.

MILTON'S POETICAL WORKS. Edited with Text collated from the best Authorities, with Introduction and Notes, by DAVID MASSON. Three Vols 8vo. 42s. With three Portraits engraved by C. H. JEENS. (Uniform with the Cambridge Shakespeare.) Fcap. 8vo Edition. With Portraits. Three Vols. 15s. (Globe Edition.) By the same Editor. Globe 8vo. 3s. 6d.

MISTRAL (F.).—MIRELLE, a Pastoral Epic of Provence. Translated by H. CRICHTON. Extra fcap. 8vo. 6s.

MITFORD (A. B.).—TALES OF OLD JAPAN. By A. B. MITFORD, Second Secretary to the British Legation in Japan. With Illustrations drawn and cut on Wood by Japanese Artists. New and Cheaper Edition. Crown 8vo. 6s.

MOLESWORTH.—Works by Mrs. MOLESWORTH (ENNIS GRAHAM).

ROSY. Illustrated by WALTER CRANE. Globe 8vo. 4s. 6d.

SUMMER STORIES FOR BOYS AND GIRLS. Crown 8vo. 4s. 6d.

THE ADVENTURES OF HERR BABY. By Mrs. MOLESWORTH, Author of "Carrots," &c. With Twelve full-page Pictures by WALTER CRANE. Globe 4to. 6s.

GRANDMOTHER DEAR. Illustrated by WALTER CRANE. Globe 8vo, gilt. 4s. 6d.

TELL ME A STORY. Illustrated by WALTER CRANE. Globe 8vo, gilt. 4s. 6d.

"CARROTS"; JUST A LITTLE BOY. Illustrated by WALTER CRANE. Globe 8vo, gilt. 4s. 6d.

THE CUCKOO CLOCK. Illustrated by WALTER CRANE. Globe 8vo, gilt. 4s. 6d.

THE TAPESTRY ROOM. Illustrated by WALTER CRANE. Globe 8vo. 4s. 6d.

A CHRISTMAS CHILD. Illustrated by WALTER CRANE. Globe 8vo. 4s. 6d.

MORTE D'ARTHUR.—SIR THOMAS MALORY'S BOOK OF KING ARTHUR AND OF HIS NOBLE KNIGHTS OF THE ROUND TABLE. (Globe Edition.) Globe 8vo. 3s. 6d.

MOULTON.—SWALLOW FLIGHTS. Poems by LOUISE CHANDLER MOULTON. Extra fcap. 8vo. 4s. 6d.

MOULTRIE.—POEMS by JOHN MOULTRIE. Complete Edition. Two Vols. Crown 8vo. 7s. each.

Vol. I. MY BROTHER'S GRAVE, DREAM OF LIFE, &c. With Memoir by the Rev. Prebendary COLERIDGE.
Vol. II. LAYS OF THE ENGLISH CHURCH, and other Poems. With notices of the Rectors of Rugby, by M. H. BLOXHAM, F.R.A.S.

MRS. GANDER'S STORY. With Twenty-four Illustrations. Demy oblong. [Just ready.

MRS. JERNINGHAM'S JOURNAL. A Poem. Purporting to be the Journal of a Newly-married Lady. Third Edition. Fcap. 8vo. 3s. 6d.

MUDIE.—STRAY LEAVES. By C. E. MUDIE. New Edition. Extra fcap. 8vo. 3s. 6d. Contents:—"His and Mine"—"Night and Day"—"One of Many," &c.

MURRAY.—ROUND ABOUT FRANCE. By E. C. Grenville Murray Crown 8vo. 7s. 6d.

MYERS (ERNEST).—Works by Ernest Myers.

THE PURITANS. Extra fcap. 8vo, cloth. 2s. 6d.

POEMS. Extra fcap. 8vo. 4s. 6d.

MYERS (F. W. H.).—Works by F. W. H. Myers.

ST. PAUL. A Poem. New Edition. Extra fcap. 8vo. 2s. 6d.

THE RENEWAL OF YOUTH, and other Poems. Crown 8vo. 7s. 6d.

NADAL.—ESSAYS AT HOME AND ELSEWHERE. By E. S. Nadal. Crown 8vo. 6s.

NICHOL.—Works by John Nichol, B.A., Oxon., Regius Professor of English Language and Literature in the University of Glasgow.

HANNIBAL, A HISTORICAL DRAMA. Extra fcap. 8vo. 7s. 6d.

THE DEATH OF THEMISTOCLES, AND OTHER POEMS. Extra fcap. 8vo. 7s. 6d.

NINE YEARS OLD.—By the Author of "St. Olave's," "When I was a Little Girl," &c. Illustrated by Frölich. New Edition. Globe 8vo. 2s. 6d.

NOEL.—BEATRICE AND OTHER POEMS. By the Hon. Roden Noel. Fcap. 8vo. 6s.

NOEL (LADY AUGUSTA).—Works by Lady Augusta Noel.

OWEN GWYNNE'S GREAT WORK. Cheaper Edition. Crown 8vo. 6s.

FROM GENERATION TO GENERATION. Crown 8vo. 6s.

NORTON.—Works by the Hon. Mrs. Norton.

THE LADY OF LA GARAYE. With Vignette and Frontispiece. Eighth Edition. Fcap. 8vo. 4s. 6d.

OLD SIR DOUGLAS. New Edition. Crown 8vo. 6s.

OLIPHANT.—Works by Mrs. Oliphant.

THE LITERARY HISTORY OF ENGLAND in the end of the Eighteenth and beginning of the Nineteenth Century. Cheaper Issue. With a New Preface. 3 Vols. Demy 8vo. 21s.

AGNES HOPETOUN'S SCHOOLS AND HOLIDAYS. New Edition, with Illustrations. Globe 8vo. 2s. 6d.

THE SON OF THE SOIL. New Edition. Crown 8vo. 6s.

THE CURATE IN CHARGE. Sixth Edition. Crown 8vo. 6s.

THE MAKERS OF FLORENCE : Dante, Giotto, Savonarola, and their City. With Illustrations from Drawings by Professor Delamotte, and a Steel Portrait of Savonarola, engraved by C. H. Jeens. New and Cheaper Edition with Preface. Crown 8vo. Cloth extra. 10s. 6d.

YOUNG MUSGRAVE. Cheaper Edition. Crown 8vo. 6s.

THE BELEAGUERED CITY. Cheaper Edition. Crown 8vo. 6s.

HE THAT WILL NOT WHEN HE MAY. Cheaper Edition. Crown 8vo. 6s.

DRESS. Illustrated. Crown 8vo. 2s. 6d. [Art at Home Series.

OUR YEAR. A Child's Book, in Prose and Verse. By the Author of "John Halifax, Gentleman." Illustrated by CLARENCE DOBELL. Royal 16mo. 2s. 6d.

PAGE.—THE LADY RESIDENT, by HAMILTON PAGE. Three Vols. Crown 8vo. 31s. 6d.

PALGRAVE.—Works by FRANCIS TURNER PALGRAVE, M.A., late Fellow of Exeter College, Oxford.

THE FIVE DAYS' ENTERTAINMENTS AT WENTWORTH GRANGE. A Book for Children. With Illustrations by ARTHUR HUGHES, and Engraved Title-Page by JEENS. Small 4to, cloth extra. 6s.

LYRICAL POEMS. Extra fcap. 8vo. 6s.

ORIGINAL HYMNS. Third Edition, enlarged 18mo. 1s. 6d.

VISIONS OF ENGLAND ; being a series of Lyrical Poems on Leading Events and Persons in English History. With a Preface and Notes. Crown 8vo. 7s. 6d.

GOLDEN TREASURY OF THE BEST SONGS AND LYRICS. Edited by F. T. PALGRAVE. 18mo. 4s. 6d.

SHAKESPEARE'S SONNETS AND SONGS. Edited by F. T. PALGRAVE. With Vignette Title by JEENS. (Golden Treasury Series.) 18mo. 4s. 6d.

THE CHILDREN'S TREASURY OF LYRICAL POETRY. Selected and arranged with Notes by F. T. PALGRAVE. 18mo. 2s. 6d. And in Two Parts, 1s. each.

HERRICK: SELECTIONS FROM THE LYRICAL POEMS. With Notes. (Golden Treasury Series.) 18mo. 4s. 6d.

PANSIE'S FLOUR BIN. By the Author of "When I was a Little Girl," " St. Olave's," &c. Illustrated by ADRIAN STOKES. Globe 8vo. 4s. 6d.

PATER.—THE RENAISSANCE. Studies in Art and Poetry. By WALTER PATER, Fellow of Brasenose College. Oxford. Second Edition, Revised, with Vignette engraved by C. H. JEENS. Crown 8vo. 10s. 6d.

PATMORE.—THE CHILDREN'S GARLAND, from the Best Poets. Selected and arranged by COVENTRY PATMORE. New Edition. With Illustrations by J. LAWSON. Crown 8vo. gilt. 6s (Golden Treasury Edition.) 18mo. 4s. 6d.

PEEL.—ECHOES FROM HOREB, AND OTHER POEMS. By EDMUND PEEL, Author of " An Ancient City," &c. Crown 8vo. 3s. 6d.

PEMBER.—THE TRAGEDY OF LESBOS. A Dramatic Poem. By E. H. PEMBER. Fcap. 8vo. 4s. 6d.

PEOPLE'S EDITIONS. Profusely Illustrated, medium 4to, 6d. each; or complete in One Vol., cloth, 3s.

TOM BROWN'S SCHOOL DAYS. By an Old Boy.

WATERTON'S WANDERINGS IN SOUTH AMERICA.

WASHINGTON IRVING'S OLD CHRISTMAS.

WASHINGTON IRVING'S BRACEBRIDGE HALL.

PHILLIPS (S. K.).—ON THE SEABOARD; and Other Poems. By SUSAN K. PHILLIPS. Second Edition. Crown 8vo. 5s.

PHILPOT.—A POCKET OF PEBBLES, WITH A FEW SHELLS; Being Fragments of Reflection, now and then with Cadence, made up mostly by the Sea-shore. By the Rev. W. B. PHILPOT. Second Edition, picked, sorted, and polished anew; with Two Illustrations by GEORGE SMITH. Fcap. 8vo. 5s.

PLATO.—THE REPUBLIC OF. Translated into English with Notes by J. LL, DAVIES, M.A., and D. J. VAUGHAN, M.A. (Golden Treasury Series.) 18mo. 4s. 6d.

POEMS OF PLACES—(ENGLAND AND WALES). Edited by H. W. LONGFELLOW. (Golden Treasury Series.) 18mo. 4s. 6d.

POETS (ENGLISH).—SELECTIONS, with Critical Introduction by various writers, and a general Introduction by MATTHEW ARNOLD. Edited by T. H. WARD, M.A. Four Vols. Crown 8vo 7s. 6d. each.

Vol. I. CHAUCER TO DONNE.

Vol. II. BEN JONSON TO DRYDEN.

Vol. III. ADDISON TO BLAKE.

Vol. IV. WORDSWORTH TO SYDNEY DOBELL

POOLE.—PICTURES OF COTTAGE LIFE IN THE WEST OF ENGLAND. By MARGARET E. POOLE. New and Cheaper Edition. With Frontispiece by R. FARREN. Crown 8vo. 3s. 6d.

POPE.—POETICAL WORKS OF. Edited with Notes and Introductory Memoir by ADOLPHUS WILLIAM WARD, M.A. (Globe Edition.) Globe 8vo. 3s. 6d.

POPULATION OF AN OLD PEAR TREE. From the French of E. VAN BRUYSSEL. Edited by the Author of "The Heir of Redclyffe." With Illustrations by BECKER. Cheaper Edition. Crown 8vo, gilt. 4s. 6d.

POTTER.—LANCASHIRE MEMORIES. By LOUISA POTTER. Crown 8vo. 6s.

PRINCE FLORESTAN OF MONACO, THE FALL OF. By HIMSELF. New Edition, with Illustration and Map. 8vo, cloth extra. gilt edges. 5s. A French Translation. 5s. Also an Edition for the People. Crown 8vo. 1s.

PUSHKIN.—EUGENE ONÉGUINE. A Romance of Russian Life in Verse. By ALEXANDER PUSHKIN. Translated from the Russian by Lieut.-Col. SPALD-ING. Crown 8vo. 6s.

RACHEL OLLIVER.—A Novel. Three Vols. Crown 8vo. 31s. 6d.

REALMAH.—By the Author of "Friends in Council. Crown 8vo. 6s.

RHOADES.—POEMS. By JAMES RHOADES. Fcap. 8vo. 4s. 6d.

RICHARDSON.—THE ILIAD OF THE EAST. A Selection of Legends drawn from Valmiki's Sanskrit Poem, "The Ramayana." By FREDERIKA RICHARDSON. Crown 8vo. 7s. 6d.

ROBINSON CRUSOE. Edited with Biographical Introduction by HENRY KINGSLEY. (Globe Edition.) Globe 8vo. 3*s*. 6*d*.—Golden Treasury Edition. Edited by J. W. CLARK, M.A. 18mo. 4*s*. 6*d*.

ROSSETTI.—Works by CHRISTINA ROSSETTI.

POEMS. Complete Edition, containing "Goblin Market," "The Prince's Progress," &c. With Four Illustrations. Extra fcap. 8vo. 6*s*.

SPEAKING LIKENESSES. Illustrated by ARTHUR HUGHES. Crown 8vo, gilt edges. 4*s*. 6*d*.

A PAGEANT, AND OTHER POEMS. Extra fcap. 8vo. 6*s*.

RUTH AND HER FRIENDS. A Story for Girls. With a Frontispiece. New Edition. Globe 8vo. 2*s*. 6*d*.

SCOURING OF THE WHITE HORSE; OR, THE LONG VACATION RAMBLE OF A LONDON CLERK. By the Author of "Tom Brown's School Days." Illustrated by DOYLE. Imp. 16mo. Cloth gilt. 5*s*.

SCOTT (SIR WALTER).—POETICAL WORKS OF. Edited with a Biographical and Critical Memoir by FRANCIS TURNER PALGRAVE. (Globe Edition.) Globe 8vo. 3*s*. 6*d*.

SCOTTISH SONG.—A SELECTION OF THE CHOICEST LYRICS OF SCOTLAND. By MARY CARLYLE AITKEN. (Golden Treasury Series.) 18mo. 4*s*. 6*d*.

SELBORNE (LORD).—THE BOOK OF PRAISE. From the best English Hymn writers. (Golden Treasury Series.) 18mo. 4*s*. 6*d*.

SERMONS OUT OF CHURCH. By the Author of "John Halifax, Gentleman." Crown 8vo. 6*s*.

SHAKESPEARE.—The Works of WILLIAM SHAKESPEARE. Cambridge Edition. Edited by W. GEORGE CLARK, M.A., and W. ALDIS WRIGHT, M.A. Nine Vols. 8vo, cloth.

SHAKESPEARE'S COMPLETE WORKS. Edited, by W. G. CLARK, M.A., and W. ALDIS WRIGHT, M.A. (Globe Edition.) Globe 8vo. 3*s*. 6*d*.

SHAKESPEARE'S SONGS AND SONNETS. Edited, with Notes, by FRANCIS TURNER PALGRAVE. (Golden Treasury Series.) 18mo. 4*s*. 6*d*.

SHAKESPEARE PHRASE BOOK, THE. By JOHN BARTLETT, Author of "Familiar Quotations." Globe 8vo. 12*s*. 6*d*.

SHAKESPEARE'S PLAYS. An attempt to determine the Chronological Order. By the Rev. H. PAINE STOKES, B.A. Extra fcap. 8vo. 4*s*. 6*d*.

SHAKESPEARE'S TEMPEST. Edited, with Glossarial and Explanatory Notes, by the Rev. J. M. JEPHSON. New Edition. 18mo. 1s.

SHORTHOUSE.—JOHN INGLESANT: A ROMANCE. By J. H. SHORTHOUSE. 2 Vols. *New and Cheaper Edition.* Globe 8vo. 12s.

SHELLEY.—POEMS OF. Edited by STOPFORD A. BROOKE. (Golden Treasury Series.) 18mo. 4s. 6d. Also a fine Edition printed on hand-made paper. Crown 8vo. 12s. 6d.

SMEDLEY.—TWO DRAMATIC POEMS. By MENELLA BUTE SMEDLEY. Author of "Lady Grace," &c. Extra fcap. 8vo. 6s.

SMITH.—POEMS. By CATHERINE BARNARD SMITH. Fcap. 8vo. 5s.

SMITH.—Works by Rev. WALTER C. SMITH.

HYMNS OF CHRIST AND THE CHRISTIAN LIFE. Fcap 8vo. 6s.

HILDA AMONG THE BROKEN GODS. Third Edition. Fcap. 8vo. 7s. 6d.

SMITH.—THREE ENGLISH STATESMEN, A Course of Lectures on the Political History of England. By GOLDWIN SMITH. New Edition. Crown 8vo. 5s.

SONG BOOK. WORDS AND TUNES FROM THE BEST POETS AND MUSICIANS. Selected and arranged by JOHN HULLAH. (Golden Treasury Series.) 18mo. 4s. 6d.

SPENSER.—COMPLETE WORKS OF. Edited by the Rev. R. MORRIS, M.A., LL.D., with a Memoir by J. W. HALES, M.A. (Globe Edition.) Globe 8vo. 3s. 6d.

STEPHEN (C. E.).—THE SERVICE OF THE POOR; being an Inquiry into the Reasons for and against the Establishment of Religious Sisterhoods for Charitable Purposes. By CAROLINE EMILIA STEPHEN. Crown 8vo. 6s. 6d.

STREETS AND LANES OF A CITY: Being the Reminiscences of AMY DUTTON. With a Preface by the BISHOP OF SALISBURY. Second and Cheaper Edition. Globe 8vo. 2s. 6d.

TANNER.—THE ABBOTT'S FARM: or, PRACTICE WITH SCIENCE. By HENRY TANNER, M.R.A.C., F.C.S., late Professor of Principles of Agriculture in the Royal Agricultural College; Examiner in the Principles of Agriculture under the Government Department of Science. Author of "First Principles of Agriculture," &c. Extra fcap. 8vo. 3s. 6d.

THE RUNAWAY. By the Author of "Mrs. Jerningham's Journal." With Illustrations. Globe 8vo. 2s. 6d.

THIRTY YEARS.—BEING POEMS NEW AND OLD. By the Author of "John Halifax, Gentleman." New Edition. Crown 8vo. 6s

THOMPSON. —A HANDBOOK TO THE PUBLIC PICTURE GAL-LERIES OF EUROPE. With a brief sketch of the History of the various Schools of Painting from the thirteenth century to the eighteenth, inclusive. By KATE THOMPSON. Third Edition, Revised and Enlarged. With numerous Illustrations. Crown 8vo. 7s. 6d.

THROUGH THE RANKS TO A COMMISSION.—*New and Cheaper Edition.* Crown 8vo. 2s. 6d.

TOM BROWN'S SCHOOL DAYS. By AN OLD BOY. With Seven Illustrations by A. HUGHES and SYDNEY HALL. Crown 8vo. 6s. ; Golden Treasury Edition. 4s. 6d.; People's Edition. 2s. People's Sixpenny Illustrated Edition. Medium 4to. 6d.

TOM BROWN AT OXFORD. New Edition. With Illustrations. Crown 8vo. 6s.

TOURGÉNIEF.—VIRGIN SOIL. By I. TOURGÉNIEF. Translated by ASHTON W. DILKE. Cheaper Edition. Crown 8vo. 6s.

TRENCH. —Works by R. CHENEVIX TRENCH, D.D., Archbishop of Dublin (For other Works by this Author, see THEOLOGICAL, HISTORICAL, and PHILO-SOPHICAL CATALOGUES.)

POEMS. Collected and arranged anew. Fcap. 8vo. 7s. 6d.

HOUSEHOLD BOOK OF ENGLISH POETRY. Selected and arranged, with Notes, by Archbishop TRENCH. Third Edition, revised. Extra fcap. 8vo. 5s. 6d.

SACRED LATIN POETRY, Chiefly Lyrical. Selected and arranged for Use. By Archbishop TRENCH. Third Edition, Corrected and Improved. Fcap. 8vo. 7s.

TYRWHITT.—OUR SKETCHING CLUB. Letters and Studies on Land-scape Art. By the Rev. R. ST. JOHN TYRWHITT, M.A. With an Authorised Reproduction of the Lessons and Woodcuts in Professor Ruskin's "Elements of Drawing." Second Edition. Crown 8vo. 7s. 6d.

UNDER THE LIMES. By the Author of "Christina North." Second Edition. Crown 8vo. 6s.

VIRGIL.—THE WORKS OF. Rendered into English Prose. By JOHN LONSDALE, M.A., and SAMUEL LEE, M.A. (Globe Edition.) Globe 8vo. 3s. 6d.

WARD.—ENGLISH POETS. Selections, with Critical Introductions by various writers, and a general Introduction by MATTHEW ARNOLD. Edited by T. H. WARD, M.A. Four Vols. Crown 8vo. 7s. 6d. each.

Vol. I. CHAUCER TO DONNE.

Vol. II. BEN JONSON TO DRYDEN.

Vol. III. ADDISON TO BLAKE.

Vol. IV. WORDSWORTH TO SYDNEY DOBELL.

WARD, MRS. T. H.—MILLY AND OLLY ; or, a Holiday among the Mountains. By Mrs. T. H. WARD. Illustrated by Mrs. ALMA TADEMA. Globe 8vo. 2s. 6d.

WEBSTER.—Works by AUGUSTA WEBSTER.

DRAMATIC STUDIES. Extra fcap. 8vo. 5s.

A WOMAN SOLD, AND OTHER POEMS. Crown 8vo. 7s. 6d

PORTRAITS. Second Edition. Extra fcap. 8vo. 3s. 6d.

MEDEA OF EURIPIDES. Literally translated into English Verse. Extra fcap. 8vo. 3s. 6d.

THE AUSPICIOUS DAY. A Dramatic Poem. Extra fcap. 8vo. 5s.

YU-PE-YA'S LUTE. A Chinese Tale in English Verse. Extra fcap. 8vo. 3s. 6d.

A HOUSEWIFE'S OPINIONS. Crown 8vo. 7s. 6d.

A BOOK OF RHYME. Crown 8vo. 3s. 6d.

WHEN I WAS A LITTLE GIRL. By the Author of " St. Olaves."
Illustrated by L. FRÖLICH. Globe 8vo. 2s. 6d.

WHEN PAPA COMES HOME : The Story of Tip, Tap, Toe. By
the Author of " Nine Years Old," " Pansie's Flour Bin," &c. With Illustrations
by W. J. HENNESSY. Globe 8vo. 4s. 6d.

WHITE.—RHYMES BY WALTER WHITE. 8vo. 7s. 6d.

WHITTIER.—JOHN GREENLEAF WHITTIER'S POETICAL WORKS.
Complete Edition, with Portrait engraved by C. H. JEENS. 18mo. 4s. 6d.

WILLOUGHBY.—FAIRY GUARDIANS. A Book for the Young By
F. WILLOUGHBY. Illustrated. Crown 8vo, gilt 5s.

WOLF.—THE LIFE AND HABITS OF WILD ANIMALS. Twenty
Illustrations by JOSEPH WOLF, engraved by J. W. and E. WHYMPER. With
descriptive Letter-press by D. G. ELLIOT, F.L.S. An Edition in royal folio,
Proofs before Letters, each Proof signed by the Engravers.

WOOLNER.—Works by THOMAS WOOLNER, R.A.

MY BEAUTIFUL LADY. With a Vignette by A. HUGHES. Third Edition
Fcap. 8vo. 5s.

PYGMALION. A Poem. Crown 8vo. 7s 6d.

WORDS FROM THE POETS. Selected by the Editor of " Ray
of Sunlight." With a Vignette and Frontispiece. 18mo, limp. 1s.

WORDSWORTH.—SELECT POEMS OF. Chosen and Edited, with
Preface, by MATTHEW ARNOLD. (Golden Treasury Series.) 18mo. 4s. 6d.
Fine Edition. Crown 8vo, hand-made paper, with Portrait of Wordsworth
engraved by C. H. JEENS, and Printed on India Paper. 9s.

YONGE (C. M.).—New Illustrated Edition of Novels and Tales by CHARLOTTE M. YONGE.

In Eighteen Volumes. Crown 8vo. 6*s*. each:—

Vol. I. THE HEIR OF REDCLYFFE. With Illustrations by KATE GREENAWAY.

II. HEARTSEASE. With Illustrations by KATE GREENAWAY.

III. HOPES AND FEARS. With Illustrations by HERBERT GANDY.

IV. DYNEVOR TERRACE. With Illustrations by ADRIAN STOKES.

V. THE DAISY CHAIN. Illustrated by J. P. ATKINSON.

VI. THE TRIAL. Illustrated by J. P. ATKINSON.

VII. & VIII. THE PILLARS OF THE HOUSE; or, UNDER WODE, UNDER RODE. Illustrated by HERBERT GANDY. Two Vols.

IX. THE YOUNG STEPMOTHER. New Edition. Illustrated by MARIAN HUXLEY.

X. CLEVER WOMAN OF THE FAMILY. New Edition. Illustrated by ADRIAN STOKES.

XI. THE THREE BRIDES. Illustrated by ADRIAN STOKES.

XII. MY YOUNG ALCIDES: or, A FADED PHOTOGRAPH. Illustrated by ADRIAN STOKES.

XIII. THE CAGED LION. Illustrated by W. J. HENNESSY.

XIV. THE DOVE IN THE EAGLE'S NEST. Illustrated by W. J. HENNESSY.

XV. THE CHAPLET OF PEARLS; or, THE WHITE AND BLACK RIBAUMONT. Illustrated by W. J. HENNESSY.

XVI. LADY HESTER AND THE DANVERS PAPERS. Illustrated by JANE E. COOK.

XVII. MAGNUM BONUM: or, MOTHER CAREY'S BROOD. Illustrated by W. J. HENNESSY.

XVIII. LOVE AND LIFE. Illustrated by W. J HENNESSY.

YONGE (C.M.).—Works by CHARLOTTE M. YONGE:—

UNKNOWN TO HISTORY. A Novel. 2 Vols. Crown 8vo. 9*s*.

THE PRINCE AND THE PAGE. A Tale of the Last Crusade. Illustrated. New Edition. Globe 8vo. 4*s*. 6*d*.

THE LANCES OF LYNWOOD. New Edition. With Illustrations. 18mo. 4*s*. 6*d*.

THE LITTLE DUKE: RICHARD THE FEARLESS. New Edition. Illustrated. Globe 8vo. 4*s*. 6*d*.

YONGE (C. M.)—*continued.*

A BOOK OF GOLDEN DEEDS OF ALL TIMES AND ALL COUN-
TRIES, Gathered and Narrated Anew. (Golden Treasury Series.) 4*s*. 6*d*.
Cheap Edition. 1*s*.

LITTLE LUCY'S WONDERFUL GLOBE. Illustrated by L. Frölich.
Globe 8vo. 4*s*. 6*d*.

A BOOK OF WORTHIES. (Golden Treasury Series.) 18mo. 4*s*. 6*d*.

THE STORY OF THE CHRISTIANS AND MOORS IN SPAIN.
(Golden Treasury Series.) 18mo. 4*s*. 6*d*.

CAMEOS FROM ENGLISH HISTORY, From Rollo to Edward II.
Third Edition, enlarged. Extra fcap. 8vo.

Second Series. THE WARS IN FRANCE. New Edition. Extra fcap.
8vo. 5*s*.

Third Series. THE WARS OF THE ROSES. Extra fcap. 8vo. 5*s*.

Fourth Series. REFORMATION TIMES. Extra fcap. 8vo. 5*s*.

P's and Q's; or, THE QUESTION OF PUTTING UPON. With Illustrations by C. O. Murray. New Edition. Globe 8vo, cloth gilt. 4*s*. 6*d*.

BYEWORDS: A COLLECTION OF TALES NEW AND OLD. Crown 8vo,
6*s*.